MW01243601

CONTENTS

RESCUE BEAR

P.O.L.A.R.

CANDACE AYERS

LOVESTRUCK ROMANCE

AUTHOR'S NOTE

***P.O.L.A.R.** (**P**rivate **O**ps: **L**eague **A**rctic **R**escue) is a specialized, private operations task force—a maritime unit of polar bear shifters. Part of a world-wide, clandestine army comprised of the best of the best shifters, P.O.L.A.R.'s home base is Siberia...until the team pisses somebody off and gets re-assigned to Sunkissed Key, Florida and these arctic shifters suddenly find themselves surrounded by sun, sand, flip-flops and palm trees.*

One week.

That's all it took for Megan's world to fall apart.

She lost everything.

Her marriage—shattered.
Her business—demolished.
Her life—ruined.

Enter one hot Rescue Bear to pick up the pieces,
build her back up,
and shower her with the love she's never known and always deserved.

1

MEGAN

I knew before I walked any further into my house that I was about to become a cliché. Wife walks in on husband sleeping with someone else, wife screams and cries and tears at her hair. Husband, wearing a sheet and nothing else, chases angry wife and apologizes profusely as she runs out of the bedroom. There was nothing original about the scene that was about to play out.

I listened to the loud moans, the grunting, the rhythmic knocking of my bedframe into the wall behind it. I couldn't remember the last time I'd been in the room as that bedframe rhythmically knocked into the wall.

I stood at the bottom of the staircase staring at the framed photos that hung on the wall in the hallway just outside our bedroom door. I'd taken each one with care—capturing just the right lighting and angles in each of them. I'd managed to make Dylan look broader and "manlier" while also making myself look smaller and daintier. That hadn't been easy. Then, after selecting the best proofs, I'd obsessed over the perfect matting and frame selection. Weeks of work had gone into the grouping on the wall. A thin layer of dust coated the top of each of the frames.

The third stair always creaked. I skipped it as I climbed. I'd been meaning to fix it. It probably just needed a couple of screws to secure it. I'd refinished the staircase myself last year, but it probably still needed a little work. Just like the railing by the sixth step. The underside could use another sanding and a reapplication of stain. Those things were just a couple of the small projects on my list—a list that kept growing longer and longer. With no time to do anything but work in the shop that Dylan and I owned, the house had been somewhat neglected.

Our bedroom door was ajar. A crumpled shirt on the floor, one that I recognized, had blocked it from fully closing. Or so it appeared. I'd ironed that shirt for Dylan just this morning. Now, crumpled carelessly on the floor with a button missing, it told a story of fevered passion. Said button was next to it, resting face down, possibly in shame of what was occurring on the bed nearby.

Further into the room, were two pairs of pants, entwined. Another shirt, significantly smaller. It'd always bothered me that my shirts weren't much smaller than Dylan's. Really, it was only the cut that made them appear smaller. Beyond the tiny shirt, tiny underwear on the floor next to Dylan's boxers. His socks. Why had he taken his socks off last? It would've made him look so stupid. The nude male body in just a pair of black cotton dress socks looked ridiculous.

Standing outside of my bedroom door like some sort of burglar or peeping Tom, I was too afraid to lift my eyes from the clothing trail to the bed. It was the bed Dylan's mother, Sandy, had gifted us. It was some fancy thing that came with remotes and a built-in heating system. Why we needed that in Florida, I'd never know. The sheets, I'd picked out while visiting my brother in DC. His wife and I had gone on a shopping trip for the perfect bedding for my very first co-owned bed. Something soft, but not too feminine for Dylan's taste.

The sounds grew louder. I felt like a third wheel, the only person in the room not caught in the throes of passion. Why did I feel like the intruder? It was *my* house. I had this weird feeling I'd walked into someone else's home and was witnessing their personal moment. Two lovers, bound together, unaware of the unwanted spectator edging her way in. Why in the world I felt guilty was beyond me.

When I forced my gaze higher, my eyes landed on a petite, shapely back. A small mole dotted her right shoulder and an even tan went all the way down the slim waist with no visible tan lines. Blonde hair bounced wildly from a ponytail, my husband's hand entangled in it as they rocked together. His hand, a part of him that I'd always found so attractive, was a shade darker than her tan, the golden hairs dusting it just so. It was a beautiful hand, strong and well formed. I loved that hand.

My carefully selected sheets were bunched at the end of the bed, the light duvet on the floor by Dylan's socks. From my angle, I could see everything. Dylan's legs, his paler feet digging into the mattress, pumping his hips upward. The owner of the beautiful back had her small feet planted on either side of my husband's thighs, her toes curling. Her tight ass, her perfect curves, their joining, I could see it all.

I could see everything but Dylan's face. His handsome face was obscured by her body, his voice muffled as he grunted a name I didn't recognize. That same face that had smiled at me that midmorning when he told me he had to step out of the shop to run some errands. As it pertained to the business side of the shop we owned, I wouldn't understand it, of course. No need to worry my little brain about it. That face that had kissed my chin, an awkward miss of a kiss that I hadn't thought to laugh at, was buried in the chest of a woman with perfect curves, a beautiful back, and a tight ass. It was calling out another's woman's name as he reached orgasm. It hadn't been so long that I didn't recognize the sound of his orgasm.

Just to the side of their clutched hands, over on the nightstand, was a picture of me and Dylan on our first date. Ten years earlier, at a pizza shop. He'd wanted pepperoni. I'd wanted sausage. We'd gotten pepperoni. A younger, more naive version of my own face stared out from the picture frame and onto what was happening on the bed, her smile appearing strained even then. Maybe she knew deep down. Next to her, Dylan. Dylan, always charming. Dylan, never wrong. Dylan, best boyfriend and worst husband. *My* Dylan.

Groaning and ruffling of the sheets drew my attention back to my bed, and I watched as beautiful back rolled off of my husband and curled into his side. They spoke to each other with the breathiness of an orgasm's afterglow, still unaware of my presence.

I didn't want to be a cliché. I didn't want to be the wife who found her husband in their bed with another woman. I didn't want any of it.

I was never the type to run from problems, though. I squared my shoulders, shoulders much broader than those of the petite woman lying naked next to my husband, and cleared my throat. My voice was steady and clear.

"We should probably talk, huh?"

2

ROMAN

Sunkissed Key was about as hot as the fires of hell. It would've been scorching even if I wasn't a polar bear shifter accustomed to frigid climates. As it was, I was melting into the ground. I couldn't remember a time since we'd arrived that I hadn't been sweat-soaked. My bear absolutely hated this miserable hellhole.

Our P.O.L.A.R. office on Main Street had two window air-conditioning units. The damn things blew a stream of cold air about two feet forward in a straight line, never actually dispersing it throughout the room or cooling much of anything down. Only when I stood directly in front of them did I find any sort of relief. Then, I had to deal with listening to the others bitch about blocking the cool air.

P.O.L.A.R. was our private ops task force, a specialized, clandestine unit within a worldwide army of shifters. Our unit name: League Arctic Rescue. There were six of us in our unit: Serge, Maxim, Dmitry, Alexei, Konstantin, and me. The "Arctic" part of "League Arctic Rescue" meant that we were usually based in a colder climate—Siberia, to be specific—where the daytime temperature didn't plaster our thick fur to our bodies while we drowned in our own perspiration.

Due to a little screwup, we found ourselves abruptly transferred to what could accurately be described as Dante's butthole on Earth—Sunkissed Key, Florida.

A month had passed and none of us had gotten acclimatized. It was mid-September and showing no signs of cooling off. Swimming in the vast expanses of the Atlantic Ocean and the Gulf of Mexico helped, but as soon as we stepped out of the water, the hot sun beat down mercilessly.

I was sitting under one of the AC units in the office when we got the first hurricane warning. It wasn't the biggest surprise. Something had felt off for days, and the way the pressure in the air shifted over our fur had been mentioned a few times. When headquarters sent us the memo, it all made sense. It would be our first hurricane, and I couldn't help but get a little excited.

We were used to doing real private operations work in Siberia—infiltrating organized crime, ensnaring double agents, doing the dirty jobs that government agencies didn't keep paperwork on. The only thing we'd done since arriving in Sunkissed Key was break up bar fights, dissolve domestic squabbles, and drip sweat. The prospect of real danger was almost like an icy cool breeze. Almost.

Serge, the team leader of P.O.L.A.R., stood and walked over to the printer. After a few seconds, the thing spat out a sheet of paper which he snatched up. He scanned it and thumped it, just as excited as the rest of us. "It's about a week out. Looks like its path is going to slam right into us—head on, boys."

Dmitry stood up and nodded. "Okay."

"How do we prepare for a hurricane?" Alexei looked around the office like he was going to find a prep kit at his feet. "I mean, I've watched *Gilligan's Island* and all, but I'm not sure we can tie everyone on this island to a tree."

"They didn't tie themselves to trees." I frowned. "Did they?"

Serge shook his head. "It makes no difference what a bunch of actors did in a zany sixties sitcom. We're getting off track here. Can we focus, please?"

"I'll call headquarters for detailed instructions," I offered. "They hate me slightly less than they hate you bunch."

Maxim snorted. "That's only because your sister works in the main office."

Shrugging, I reached for the phone, but Serge was faster. He pointed the mouthpiece at me and smirked. "Too slow. I love pissing off headquarters. It's what I live for. You useless SOBs scout the island and find out what the locals do in these situations. God knows they've been through this before."

I scowled at Serge, not thrilled about being sent out in the heat. Even though the air conditioners sucked, they were better than the outdoors and straight sunshine. "Should I remind you that we're here, on this flaming head of a matchstick, because of you?"

He just laughed. "Yet, somehow, I'm still the boss and I still outrank you."

My bear didn't like the reminder that someone else outranked him. It was always an issue in our league. We were all dominant brawlers, and our animals tended to be loners. Each one of us knew logically that in order for the unit to work efficiently, we needed to kowtow to an alpha, but knowing it was one thing. Doing it wasn't as easy.

Despite getting us banished to Florida, Serge was a good bear, a great soldier, and an even better man. He had never led us wrong in all the years he'd been our unit leader.

Konstantin stood up from his spot in the corner of the office and stretched. He never said much, and that moment was no exception. He just silently left the office and shut the door behind him just as quietly. He was like a ghost most days.

Alexei groaned. "I'll follow Ghost. He freaks the locals out when he's alone."

Maxim scooted his chair up to his computer. He was the techie of the league. "I've got this. Nothing that Google can't provide answers for."

With nothing left to do in the office, I sighed. Outside, it was. I clapped Dmitry on the shoulder as I passed him and used my best Austrian accent. "I'll be back."

Opening the door and stepping outside, I felt like a casserole stepping into a preheated oven. I shielded my eyes and squinted around at my surroundings.

Our P.O.L.A.R. office was in a rented office space at the southern tip of the island. The last building before the island sloped into a sandy beach leading to the ocean. The view was stunning. Ocean as far as I could see, which, for a polar bear shifter, was far. It was a picturesque place and, if it wasn't so miserably hot, it would've been a nice place for a vacation.

Sunkissed Key was a three-mile stretch of land with one main road splitting it into two halves. Business controlled most of Main Street, from one end to the other, with homes dotting smaller roads that split off it. There was a lot of beach, a lot of beauty, and a lot of vulnerable areas if the hurricane did come at us head on.

It was probably unwise to be excited about the idea of a hurricane coming. Lord knew I didn't want anyone to get hurt or killed, but we were specially trained bears, built to fight and trained to rescue. And, we were slowly dying on this island. If the heat didn't kill us, the boredom surely would. We all could do with a little excitement.

Plus, we would each do everything in our power to ensure the safety of the island's residents. We were the best of the best—highly-trained, adept operatives. If need be, we would protect our charges with our very lives.

3

MEGAN

I sat on the top step of our staircase and waited for Dylan and his mistress to get dressed. Their hushed whispers were a one-eighty from their former passionate cries. I could hear parts of what they were saying. Dylan was shocked that I wasn't at the shop. She was mad at Dylan for putting her in such an awkward situation. He was pissed at me—for coming home. It was great stuff, really.

A few minutes later, she rushed past me on the stairs. She didn't look back. I never even got a good look at her face, although I imagined she was as stunning from the front as she was from the back. Even her voice was attractive.

Dylan was slower to emerge. He even took a shower first. I glanced at my watch a few times, wondering how long he was going to drag this whole thing out. The shop was closed while we were both away. He had to know that. Normally, he had a tantrum if we left the shop closed for longer than fifteen minutes.

I sat there, my elbows resting on my knees and my chin in my hands. I didn't know what I was feeling. My mind was racing with stupid thoughts that made no sense. I couldn't stop thinking about all of the projects I needed to finish around the house and about how much there was on my to-do list.

I expected anger to bubble up at some point—or sadness. My husband had cheated on me. In our own house, in our own bed, while I was off working at *our* business that *he* insisted we open. Yet, instead of being incensed, which would have been the logical response, I sat there picking at my nails wondering when Dylan would emerge from the bedroom. As each minute ticked by, nothing. And I just couldn't stop thinking about all I needed to do.

"Megan..." Dylan's voice had the same edge to it that it always had. Nothing gentle about him, it was like he'd been fighting the world since the day he was born. "Who's at the shop?"

I watched as he skirted around me, descended and stood at the landing at the bottom of the stairs. The entry table beside him needed to be refinished. I'd picked it up at a flea market and it needed some love.

"Megan?"

I looked at my husband and squinted. I recognized the man standing there, but I didn't. Appearance-wise, he was the same. He looked like the man in the photos taken on our wedding day, but he wasn't. There was something in his expression that hadn't been there before. A slight curl to his lip, the wrinkle of his nose, as though he'd smelled something distasteful.

"Come on, Megan. What? Are you really going to give me the silent treatment? Talk to me. You're not a child."

It was me. I was the something distasteful that made his lip curl and his nose wrinkle. I ran my tongue over my teeth, searching my brain for the words that needed to be said, but I drew a blank. I didn't know what to say.

"Jesus. You want me to apologize? Fine. I'm sorry you had to see that. It's not like it's a surprise, though, right? We haven't been intimate in months."

I pulled myself to my feet and made my way down the stairs. "There's no one at the shop. I closed it to go looking for you. You weren't answering your phone, and Hurricane Matilda has altered its course. It's headed this way—expected to slam right into us."

"There's no one at the shop? Fuck, Megan. You're costing us

money that we need. What the hell were you thinking? Let's go. We need to get back."

I didn't want to be near him. I didn't know what to say to him. I wasn't ready to even try to form words from my thoughts or sentences from my words. "You go ahead. I've got stuff I need to do here."

He scowled. "You know you do all the floor stuff. That's your *job*. You can't just skip out on doing your job because we're having a bad day."

An image flashed through my mind—the image of Dylan on the floor, clutching his bloody nose after I bitch slapped the hell out of him. I had to take a step back. The urge to turn that mental image into a reality was so strong it scared me. I took another step back and then another and shook my head. "You go."

"Megan—"

"Dylan, there is nothing I want more in the world right now that to lay you out cold. I want to crack my knuckles on your face and see your nose twist the wrong way and plaster itself on the other side of your face." I balled my fists up at my sides. "The scary thing is that I'm not even angry right now. I just desperately want to see you in pain. So, I suggest you get the hell out of this house for a while. Go, work the job you swore you wanted. Or don't. I don't care. Just get out."

Looking shocked, he grabbed his keys and shook his head. "I don't know what's gotten into you."

I watched him leave and stood there until I heard his car speed away. He always drove through the neighborhood too fast. The neighbors complained to me, and I felt forced to make excuses and apologize for him, but he never felt apologetic about it and he never stopped. He said the car was meant to go fast.

I looked back down at the entry table that needed refinishing and blew out a deep sigh. It would give me something to do until I felt human again. I carefully took everything off it and placed it on the floor before carrying the table to the garage.

I was methodical in pulling out my sander and the sanding sheets. When the sander was ready, I turned it on and went to work on the table. With lots of nooks and crannies, it was a detailed job that eventually calmed my brain.

When I was alone, my solitude helped me arrive at solutions, but this time, I didn't like the solutions I came up with. Reality was staring me straight in the face and handing me some hard truths about my marriage. This truth wasn't easy to handle.

I wasn't a quitter, though. I'd made promises to Dylan and I'd meant them.

I lost all track of time, working and thinking. None of the answers I came up with made me feel any better. And, I still didn't feel sad or angry about Dylan's infidelity. What did that say about our relationship?

4

ROMAN

"This is crazy." Serge looked down the street. Standing next to the road, he posed with his hands on his hips while watching traffic slowly make its way north. "How are they all supposed to get out in time if they creep at a snail's pace?"

I stood beside him, a strange buzz starting inside of me. The energy on the island had picked up. Everyone knew something big was coming. My bear was riled up. Despite the heat, he was eager for the first time since we'd left Siberia. "I guess this is normal."

The northbound lane of Main Street was packed with cars—evacuees heading north to the mainland. Southbound was completely empty. No one dared venture farther south with Hurricane Matilda on its way. She was supposed to be big. According to the weather channel, she would be the biggest storm to hit the Keys in over a century. Unless she changed direction, she would make landfall in just under two days.

"Why didn't they leave when Matilda was first spotted? I don't know what we'll be able to do if there are this many cars still on the road when she hits."

I shrugged. "They'll be gone."

Alexei poked his head out of the office. "Upgraded to a cat five."

"Close the damn door! You're letting all the cold out." Dmitry's irritated voice rang out from inside.

Alexei, never one to follow orders, strode out of the office leaving the door wide open. In low-hanging shorts and an open shirt, he looked like a surfer. He was always laid back and easygoing, even in emergencies.

Dmitry grabbed the door and slammed it shut, grumbling the whole time.

"We should probably go around the island and encourage people to leave. See if they need any help with evacuating." Serge rolled his neck. "It makes my skin crawl to think of weak humans facing a hurricane of this expected magnitude."

I grinned as Serge's mate, Hannah, came out of the office and strolled toward him. Wrapping her very human body around his from behind, she sighed. "They're driving me crazy in there."

I could read the tension in Serge's face. He was very aware of how delicate his human mate was. He also knew she wasn't about to leave the island without him. Unless he nabbed a car and drove north, she was remaining on Sunkissed Key with the rest of us while Matilda battered the island. She was the real reason he was so anxious about the incoming storm.

To avoid hearing them argue about it again, I headed down the street, taking in the scene and trying to mentally calculate how many people were leaving versus how many would be staying. Thankfully, it seemed as though most of the island's residents would be seeking safer ground farther north. Houses were boarded up and garages and driveways were vacant of vehicles. As I scouted, whenever I came upon any of the few people still working, trying to board up their homes, I stopped to help.

The work was a far cry from the often perilous, tactical missions we'd performed while based out of Siberia, but it was something to do. I helped a few more people finish loading their cherished possessions into their cars and helped a few more cut into traffic. The little island was emptying faster by the hour. That was a good thing. People were heeding the threat. Matilda wasn't turning, nor was it growing weaker. She was headed our way with a vengeance.

I cut down Palm Street and then Parrot Cove Road to gain access to West Public Beach. The Bayfront Diner sat just off it, and Susie, who owned the place, was a sweet older woman who happily fed us cinnamon rolls and sweet tea all the time.

The sign in the window read *Closed*, but I could see Susie inside. She waved me in with a warm smile.

"Roman! Come on in, honey. I don't have anything made right now, but I can whip you up some cinnamon rolls in a jiffy." Her tall beehive of hair bobbed precariously on her head. She looked like she'd been caught in the middle of fixing it.

"What are you still doing here?" I sat across from her on a worn barstool and frowned. "You're not planning to stay, are you?"

She looked away. "I'm not planning, no. I *am* staying."

"Susie—"

"Now, Roman. I've lived on this island my entire life. I've been through rougher hurricanes than this one a-coming. I'm not leaving my diner." She reached under the counter and pulled out a coffee cup. "Coffee?"

I shook my head. "I'll watch over the place for you. No sense in you tempting fate."

"And no sense in you trying to convince a hard-headed old woman who has her mind already made up." She poured me a cup of coffee. "You need coffee. I don't care what you say. Everyone needs coffee."

I took a long sip just to be polite. I tried to ignore the fact that I was adding warmth to my already overheated body. "Where will you be bunking down for the storm?"

"Right here. My Sammy helped me build this place. It's all I've got and I ain't leaving it." She looked out through the front windows at the bay and smiled. "Although, I could use some help with boarding up the windows."

I downed the rest of my coffee and stood. "Say no more. Do you have boards, or should I go find some?"

She pointed me to the back and grasped my arm. "You're my favorite of the gang, you know that?"

It would've been a more flattering compliment if I hadn't heard her say the same thing to Alexei just last week. Still, she made me smile. "Flattery will get you everywhere."

5

MEGAN

I dragged the large sheet of plywood out of the rear of the shop and toward the front. The windows were still uncovered. It seemed that while I'd been on a hiatus from reality for the past few days, Dylan hadn't bothered to take care of closing up the shop. Every single business on the island had been boarded up. Every one but ours. Maybe he'd been too busy boning his girlfriend.

I shook my head and huffed as I stopped to take a breather. Balancing the wood against my hip, I looked around the shop dejectedly. Nothing had been put away. Nothing had been taken care of.

Dylan was sitting in the back, in his office, doing god only knew what. He was well aware that I was in the showroom—alone. Working to get the windows boarded up—alone. Did he care? Apparently not.

My anger toward him that was long overdue had been gradually coming to a simmer the last couple days. Suddenly, it threatened to boil over. "Dylan, can you *please* help?"

We hadn't spoken much since the disaster that Monday afternoon. I'd been in the garage pretty much nonstop since then, finishing each and every project on my list. I'd jumped head first into completing all the things I'd put off in exchange for working endless hours in the shop. I'd barely come up for air and, more notably, I'd avoided my husband.

My anger had grown. My sadness had not.

In truth, I didn't even know which one of us I was angrier at. Him, for being a lying, cheating backstabber, or myself for deciding not to throw in the towel.

I wasn't a quitter. I'd made vows. Together we owned a home, a business, and two cars. We'd gone through the ups and downs of life together for over ten years. I wouldn't just walk away from that at the first sign of trouble. There had to be some way to salvage our marriage.

"I'm busy, Megan." Had his voice always been so condescending and I'd just not realized it, or was that a recent development? Maybe he thought less of me for staying, too.

"This is important."

"You're strong. You can handle it." He'd barely stepped foot out of his office before he turned to go back in with a shrug of his shoulders.

"Dylan. I need help. I can't hold this board up and nail it in place, too." My voice sounded like I was forcing it out through gritted teeth. Probably because I was.

"I don't know what to tell you. That's your area. You ought to enjoy it, since that kind of thing is all you've wanted to do lately." He gestured toward the wood in my hand. "You sure have been slacking here at the shop."

"You could've had your girlfriend cover my shifts, I guess." I threw that down like a gauntlet, ready to duel it out with him if he was going to be such an asshole.

"She has a job, Megan. And don't be ridiculous. She's not going to come here and do *your* job."

"Oh, no? She seemed to like doing my job in our bed a few days ago."

"So, you want to do this now?" He nodded and walked toward me. "Granted, Brandi and I shouldn't have been in our bed, Megan, but let's face it, you haven't been meeting my needs. None of this has." He waved his hand around, gesturing to our surroundings.

My head snapped back like he'd slapped me. His indication that our shop was somehow at fault for his behavior was the breaking point. "Oh, this hasn't met your *needs*? The shop that *you* insisted we open? The shop that you begged and pleaded for, the shop you bitched about for months until I gave in? And why was that again? Because no other work around this island fit your *needs*? So, the shop we opened because you couldn't get another job not filling your *needs* either, now?"

"Geeze, you're mad because I criticized the shop? Not that I was screwing someone else in our bed? Doesn't that say it all?"

I opened my mouth to argue and then snapped it shut. Everything that was on the tip of my tongue—all the anger and vitriol that was right there ready to be spewed—was contrary to the decision I'd made. None of it would help solve our issues or heal our marriage. "Dylan, neither of us have had our needs met lately. The answer wasn't to sleep around on me, though. We should've worked it out. Together."

"Yeah, well, that's not how it played out." He turned to walk away. "I need to finish up some paperwork back here."

"No. We need to batten down the shop. It's a two-person job, Dylan. I can't do it alone."

"Stop acting as though you're helpless, Megan. You're a *big girl*."

His words—casual and flippant—tumbled from his mouth so easily, yet they hit me like a brick. The extra pounds I carried were an area of self-deprecation for me. Walking in on my husband and his mistress and seeing her petite figure with a waist the size of a child's hadn't helped my insecurities. Dylan knew all the ways I'd been teased from my teenage years on into college. I was a head taller than most of the rest of the girls and had always had a thick build.

He knew the impact the words "big girl" carried for me. Maybe it was a slip, but it was one he'd never made before.

"Fuck you."

Dylan jerked around and came at me with a furious expression twisting his face. "No, fuck you!"

I let the wood fall to the floor with a loud slap. "Why? For walking in on you? For forcing you to work in the shop alone, the same way you've made me do so many times before, probably so you could sneak off to be with another woman?"

"Oh, poor Megan. You've had it so rough, haven't you?"

I backed away. "You know what? You can close up yourself."

"Fuck that."

"Close up the shop or let everything be ruined by the storm. I don't care. I'm tired of picking up all the slack for you."

"Go to hell, Megan. This! This right here is why I have Brandi. She's not sour and bitter like you." He grabbed my upper arm and yanked me back around to face him. "You think you're so much better than me. I can see it. The way you've been acting the past few days. You think you're suddenly "holier than thou" because you didn't sleep around. But put yourself in my shoes. Married to someone who's cold and dead inside. It's like being married to a big, limp fish. Jesus, Megan, I think I hate you."

His fingers cut into me as he spoke, my arm throbbed under his grip, but I refused to flinch. I wasn't going to let him know how badly he was hurting me—both physically and emotionally. "Let me go."

He immediately released me and shook his head. "I don't know why I even try."

I laughed bitterly while rubbing my arm. "You're trying?"

He just marched back into his office and slammed the door.

I could no longer hold back the tears. Through blurred vision, I let myself out of the shop and drove home. With practically the entire island evacuating north, the southbound lane was vacant. Our home at the end of Beach Street was, appropriately, on the beach. It stood feet from the ocean on pillars. It was a beautiful home, inherited from my grandparents, and I'd nearly completely renovated it myself.

My home. No longer *our* home, if that's what I chose. I could kick Dylan out—send him on his way. There'd been a prenup involved with our marriage, even though we'd gotten married at such a young age. I came from a family with money who'd demanded it. Perhaps they'd been smarter than I was and saw the inevitable future of my marriage to Dylan that I'd been blind to.

Divorcing Dylan was an option. As I looked down at the angry red fingertip marks on my arm that were turning purplish, it didn't seem like the worst option. I hated divorce, though. My family was one with a legacy of divorces. My mother and father were each other's third and fourth spouses, respectively. Their marriage had only lasted three years. And after their divorce, each had subsequently gone through several more spouses.

I didn't want to be another family joke.

In the guest room where I'd been staying, I crawled into bed and pulled the covers over my head. Finally, I allowed the tears that had been choking me on the drive home to flow freely. Once they came, they didn't feel as though they were ever going to stop.

6

MEGAN

Sunday morning. Matilda was still heading straight for us. I'd spent the night crying into my pillow and listening for Dylan to arrive home. He never did. When my alarm went off that morning at six, the same as it did every day, the local news blared warnings about the incoming storm.

Still a category five, it didn't look as though Matilda would go easy on the islands. It took Maverick Maine, the local DJ, sounding out his last broadcast to really light a fire under me. He was leaving the island, and the station would be broadcasting the national weather service alerts until he returned. Matilda was less than eighteen hours away.

I jumped up in a panic. Shit. I hadn't done anything to protect the house. I'd been so lost in the difficulties between Dylan and me that I'd let it completely slip my mind. Ugh, stupid. I didn't take time to change or shower, I just rushed downstairs and raced out onto the beach. The water already looked choppy and agitated. It seemed to know something big was coming. The sky was dark and gray, a harbinger of dangerous weather.

Other than the wind and waves, the surrounding neighborhood was eerily silent. Most people had vacated while I was in my stupor. I ran my hands over my face and then rushed to get to work. I could lose everything if I didn't board up the house.

My fury spurred me on as I worked tirelessly. The windows had shutters that I bolted closed. The first floor of the house was surrounded by a deck so those windows were easy to access. After making sure the shutters were secure, I nailed sheets of plywood over them, ensuring the house would be as protected as possible.

The second-floor windows were more of a challenge. Those had to be accessed by a ladder and each one took entirely too long. I couldn't carry a sheet of plywood up a ladder and then hold it steady over the windows while securing it. Not without help. So I nailed a couple of planks across the shutters on the second floor, in hopes that it would be enough. By the time I finished, I was flushed and sticky with sweat. The strong breeze coming off the ocean did nothing to cool me down.

Time was passing too rapidly. It had taken hours for me to secure the house alone. Before I knew it, it was late afternoon and the sky was darkening faster than it should have been. I was still tuned into the weather broadcast, and I could hear it blasting away in the house. While Matilda had been downgraded to a category four, she was moving in more quickly than first predicted.

In a state of sheer panic, I jumped in my SUV and sped down to the shop. In the back of my mind, I was hoping that Dylan had uncharacteristically stepped up and closed up our shop. I was hoping to maybe pull up and find him still there, finishing up.

Main Street was empty. Everyone had either already evacuated or, if they'd decided to stay put, had retreated indoors. I was the only idiot on the road. It took me less than two minutes to get to the shop and what I found made my heart sink. Nothing was covered. The glass windows that lined the front of our shop were still perfectly naked and I could see right through them to the prints in the shop, still on display. They had also not been packed up or moved to a safer location.

Dylan hadn't done a damn thing. I searched my pockets for my phone but came up empty. It was wherever I'd left it the night before —probably on the guest bedroom nightstand. I slammed the car door, unlocked the shop, and headed straight to the office to grab the phone. I halted in my tracks when I saw the state of the small back room.

It was completely trashed. Empty file folders littered the floor, the desk drawers ransacked. The computer was gone, the safe under the desk was open—and empty. My hand flew to my open mouth as I sank into the office chair. I hadn't been around to do the deposit drop for a few days, but I knew we'd made several sales. I'd had some thank-you emails from customers saying they loved their new pieces. The register drawer was always placed in the safe. And it was there alright. But it was empty.

My brain reached for possibilities. We could have had a break in—been robbed. I knew the truth, though. My heart was in my toes as I reached for the phone with a shaky hand.

Dialing Dylan's number, I almost hoped he didn't answer. I didn't want to hear the truth. The reality I was facing was ugly and cruel, and I wasn't sure I could handle it while trying to take care of the business we owned together. I was devastated, not so much by the idea of losing him, more by the fact that my life was turning into a joke. I was also so furious with myself for falling into an avoidance/denial trance for the last week. I wasn't usually so lax about protecting the things I owned and cared about. I'd been through hurricanes before. I knew what to do and I'd always handled things capably and responsibly. Not this time. Waiting until last minute was not just stupid, it was dangerous. Hell, I didn't even have a decent evacuation plan.

The line clicked and Dylan's voice came through clear. "Megan."

I sank into the chair and looked up at the ceiling. It was stark white. I noticed a cobweb in a corner. "You took everything, didn't you?"

A heavy sigh. "I didn't have a choice. I needed the money."

"And the business? What? We just let it go?" My voice didn't even sound like my own. It sounded flat and vacant.

"I really don't have an answer. Maybe we should let the hurricane do its thing and collect the insurance money." He spoke to someone in the background and sighed again. "Look, Megan, you and I are over. We both know it wasn't working."

"Okay." I shook my head and sat up, feeling something unexpected pass over me—acceptance. "I guess you evacuated?"

"Yeah, of course."

If I was waiting for him to express an iota of concern for my well-being, I would have died waiting. I just dropped the phone into its cradle and looked back up at the cobweb. Something else I had only just noticed.

I couldn't afford to waste any more time. Even though I wanted to stay in that chair and obsess over how much money Dylan had taken and how he was spending it, most likely on Brandi, I couldn't. I had to take care of the shop. Just because my husband was an asshole, that didn't mean I was going to leave our shop to Matilda's wrath.

The prints hanging around the shop were worth thousands, money I would need to put back into the shop—and whatever damages Matilda wrought. I worked as fast as I could to take them down and layer them between packing blankets in the trunk of my SUV. Then I got all of the other delicate material out of the shop. The cheaper prints that I could redo if necessary, I carted into the office and stored on top of the desk, in case water did come inside.

Screwing plywood over the windows was a task for at least two people, but I managed to do an okay job of it. I had to ignore the strain on my body to get it done. Lifting and using my body to hold the boards in place while I stretched to screw in the bottom was painful and awkward, as was stretching my arms overhead to secure the top of the plywood.

The wind picked up as I went, and the sky grew darker. There were eight windows and a door that needed covering, but I was only halfway done when a gust of wind took the plywood I was holding and tossed it, end over end, down the street. The damn wind ripped it right from my hands, leaving them bloody and splintered from the rough ends of the wood.

My hair whipped around my head wildly. My oversized shirt billowed out in front of me, and my eyes stung from the salty wind.

When the rain started, goosebumps spread over my body. I'd never waited so long to evacuate, nor had I ever stayed on the island through a dangerous hurricane. I was about to experience my first time—with Matilda.

I doubted she'd go easy on me, either.

My brain worked at lightning speed to formulate a plan. I wasn't sure the house would be a safe place to ride out the storm. It was on the east side of the island, facing the Atlantic, and was where Matilda would hit first. I couldn't stay in the shop. Even if I did manage to get the rest of the windows boarded up, it wouldn't be structurally safe. I didn't know where to go. Maybe the medical center on the west side of the island. It was small but made from reinforced concrete. If I could get in, it would be safer than most places.

I turned back to the windows and, with a renewed determination, decided that I had time to finish and still make it to the medical center before the brunt of the storm hit. I went after the board that had flown down the street and got back to work.

My determination faded almost as fast as it had arrived, however, as the wind grew increasingly stronger. I was weak from the physical exertion I'd done all day—boarding up the house and then the shop—and hadn't thought to eat anything. I only got one more window done before I hit a wall. I didn't have enough energy or strength left to finish.

I stepped back from the shop and wiped at a stray tear. I felt as though life was closing a chapter on me that I hadn't planned on closing. No matter the situation, I didn't want to see the building damaged. It had been good to us.

Before I could continue my sentimental journey, a huge wind gust shoved me sideways. I caught myself and then looked east. Horrified, I saw that the shoreline was much closer than normal. The water was already coming in hard and fast. My heart raced.

I did my best to speedily shove everything in the shop higher up and farther away from the windows. When I'd done everything I could, I rushed back out and climbed in my SUV. In just the last ten minutes, the waterline had risen aggressively. I couldn't have made it back to my house, even if I'd wanted to. I floored it down Main Street to the small island medical center and parked in the ER entrance, the only place even remotely shielded from the wind and rain. I went around the back and worked quickly to pull a tarp over the prints, hoping that would offer enough protection if the windows blew out, then I closed and locked the doors.

The medical center had been evacuated early on. Maintenance had boarded the place up, protecting it from the storm and potential looters. I made my way slowly around its perimeter, searching for a way in. When I found none, I retreated to the SUV and sat in it, trying to think. I was soaked. The wind and rain rocked the vehicle; the howling made my stomach clench tightly. I didn't know where else to go. It was pitch dark by that point. The emergency broadcast system was saying that Matilda was arriving soon; a storm surge of ten to fifteen feet was expected.

It was too late to try to drive inland. It was too late to make it anywhere else. I put my head in my hands and cried. It wasn't very helpful, but I was out of options.

7

ROMAN

My bear was unusually unsettled—more so than I ever remember him being. Matilda came in with a raging attitude, beating the little island of Sunkissed Key with unbridled ferocity.

I was an adrenaline junkie—all of us in P.O.L.A.R. were—which was why we chose to do the work we did. Despite the fact that I was no stranger to hazards or risks, and I'd certainly been in more perilous situations, there was something different this time. Exciting, sure, but it also felt like something ominous was lurking just over my shoulder—something that made the hairs on the back of my neck stand on end.

The storm had just started, at a little past ten in the evening, and already, within a half hour, the east side of the island was flooded. Alexei was hanging out on a rooftop somewhere, watching and keeping us up to date. I was jealous, but I didn't want to leave Susie's. I could tell the older woman was nervous, and I wasn't about to let her face Matilda on her own.

For about the thousandth time, I stifled a growl and rolled my neck. My bear was highly agitated. "Having fun so far, Susie?"

She looked up from her find-a-word puzzle book and shrugged. "As long as my place is still standing in the morning, I'm good."

I forced a laugh and paced over to the covered windows. I wanted to see outside. I kept feeling like something was happening out there. Something I should know about, or take care of.

Anything, Alexei? I called to him through our mental link, hungry for any news.

This storm is wild! Even in my head, I could feel the energy radiating off him. *I don't know how much longer I'll stay up here, but it's been worth watching.*

See anyone in need of assistance? My bear growled again, growing even more riled. He kept urging me to go out on a rescue mission, but there was no one out there. No matter how many times I told him, and how much I tried to convince him, he just grew more determined.

No one would be crazy enough to be out in this. I think I'll head your way. Susie have any of those cinnamon rolls?

I looked over at the covered plate—what was left of the cinnamon rolls she'd made for me about twenty minutes ago. *A few. Come on. I'm going to switch positions with you for a bit. I have a weird feeling in my gut.*

Alexei showed up a few minutes later, soaked to the bone and grinning like a madman. He wiped his face and made a beeline for the cinnamon rolls. "Susie, will you marry me?"

She smiled at him. "What would you boys do without an old lady like me to look after you? Why you insist on going out in this is beyond me. It's too dangerous."

I nodded to Alexei and moved toward the door. "We'll be okay, Susie. We're trained for this kind of stuff. Come lock this behind me, Alexei. I'll let you know when I'm on my way back."

I didn't wait for them to reply. My bear was ripping at my flesh to get out and search for whatever it was that had him so worked up. I'd barely gotten ten feet from the diner before he tore free, shredding my clothing and slapping large paws down in the standing water. I lifted my head to the sky and inhaled through my elongated snout. Every one of my senses was heightened in that form, but most of all my sense of smell. I breathed deeply, searching for anything that stood out as unusual.

Salt air, island scents, and something sweet but soiled with the bitter tang of fear. My heart leaped and I ran toward the scent. A faint scream pierced the howling wind and crashing waves. Racing faster, it wasn't long before I was swimming. The surge had hit, and the island was more water than land.

Hear that? Serge came in urgent.

I've got it. Headed toward it now. I'll let you know if I need backup.

I passed the last house and felt a rip current tugging at me. I let it pull me closer to the sound of the scream. It carried me deeper into the ocean, farther south, deeper into the storm. Whoever was out there wouldn't last long. The ocean was a dangerous beast, even when not stirred up.

A flash of lightning lit up the sky, and for a split second, I saw the person. About a hundred yards out, someone was flailing to stay above the rough water. Once spotted, I was able to keep them in my sights, even in the dark. I watched as a wave crashed over them, dragging them under. My heart squeezed painfully and I pushed my muscles through the churning water.

Swimming as fast as I could, it still took me several seconds to get to the spot where I saw the person go down. It was rougher seas than I'd ever attempted to navigate before. I dove under and searched the dark waters.

A white shirt stood out and I was on it—her—in seconds. She was unconscious, and not breathing. She did not look good. My pulse raced. The idea of her not being okay was unacceptable. I had to save her. I clamped my jaw gently over her arm, being careful not to puncture her skin with my sharp teeth, and pulled her to the surface. I had to shift back to resuscitate her. The waves tossed us, and I did the best I could in the situation. One forceful blow of oxygen into her mouth and she was back with me—what a fighter.

Terrified hazel eyes flew open and connected with mine. She was frozen, her body stiff against mine.

"Are you okay?!" I shouted over the raging storm, scared I'd been too late somehow.

She blinked a few times and then looked around. Her nails bit into my skin as her hands locked onto my arms. Her legs started kicking, helping keep us afloat. She shook her head, the panic in her eyes was clear.

"I'll get us back! Just hold on to me."

I didn't give her a chance to think about it. I turned and wrapped her arms around my neck. Then, I swam like I'd never swum before. She was light on my back, but it was an awkward way to swim and I used every ounce of my shifter strength. Her mouth next to my ear was more distracting than it should've been.

She was more distracting than she should have been—especially given the dire circumstance. I was hyperaware of her body against mine. I swam hard, making sure to avoid the rip current, and got us back onto land. The land was more underwater than it had been just minutes before, but I carried her to the closest house. It was a beach house on stilts, so it was safe from the water, if not the wind.

The water level had risen halfway up the staircase. As soon as she could grab the stair railing, she let go of me and pulled herself up until she could climb the top few steps. It was easy to see that she was sluggish and weak, exhausted, and I worried.

At the top of the stairs, the home was boarded up well. I forced the door open and ushered her inside ahead of me. I'd apologize and pay for damages later. As soon as I had the door shut and secured, we were plunged into relative silence. It took a few seconds for the ringing in my ears from the howling wind and crashing waves to subside. I turned to the woman who had almost been a casualty of the storm and looked her over. The hair on the back of my neck stood on end. Tingles shot through my body.

She looked as though she was still in a daze, not quite processing reality, and that concerned me. "Are you okay? Tell me how you feel. Are you dizzy? Any trouble breathing?"

She shook her head and then nodded before shaking her head again. "I...I don't know. I don't know."

I led her over to a barstool and motioned for her to sit. When she did, I looked her over more closely. I couldn't see any damage, anything that would alert me to any injury she'd incurred. Her hazel eyes began to focus, despite everything. A just slightly upturned nose on a heart-shaped face, full lips...kissable lips. Lusciously kissable...

She coughed, her hand going over her chest.

"Do you hurt anywhere?"

"My lungs don't feel the best, but I think that's to be expected... I thought I was dead."

I didn't feel in top form myself. My bear was in a tizzy, consumed by the woman in front of us, torn between panting and growling. I didn't know what the hell was wrong with him, but I needed to gain control over him before he embarrassed me. "Anything else?

She shook her head and sank back, letting her back rest against the counter behind her. "I'm okay. I know enough about dry drowning to know that this isn't that. I'm just..."

I leaned in closer when she trailed off. She had the most delectable aroma.

"I'm just really glad you came along." When she looked up at me with those beautiful hazel eyes, I was lost in them. But then, she wrapped her arms around my neck in a tight hug.

Shocked, I hugged her in return. The gesture felt way too good—far better than a mere thank-you hug from a rescued victim. I'd had plenty of those since being recruited to the task force. No, this one triggered an immediate arousal, and I realized I'd better cover up because my downstairs was standing at full mast.

"Thank you for saving my life."

8

MEGAN

I pulled away from the man who'd rescued me and tried to ignore the awkward arousal I felt blossoming inside. I shouldn't have hugged him. How was I to know it would start my pulse racing and my body filling with lust? Maybe it was just a strange reaction to nearly dying. I coughed again and looked around the house we'd broken into. "This is Greg Campbell's house."

"A friend of yours?"

I shook my head. "Not since high school. He got this place when his parents moved to Pensacola. I was here a few times when we were kids for parties."

"Greg's really into animal print, huh?"

I looked over at the leopard-patterned pillows on the couch and bit back a laugh. "I think he's married now. Although, those could still be his, I suppose."

We grew quiet again, and I looked anywhere but at the man who'd saved me. I felt strange. When I'd regained consciousness with his mouth on mine, after thinking I was a goner, I'd assumed for a second that I'd died and gone to heaven. There was this beautiful man kissing me, or so I'd thought. I'd been ready to lean in and really kiss him back when I choked up ocean water. It was hard to hold eye contact, knowing that while he'd been trying to save my life, I'd been thinking about making out with him.

"I'm Roman." He held out his hand, and one side of his mouth lifted.

I met his eyes for a second and then slid my hand into his. I couldn't help but notice how much larger his hand was than mine. The guy was huge. "Megan."

"What were you doing out in this storm, Megan?"

I pulled my hand back from his and stood up. On shaky legs, I rounded Greg's kitchen island and occupied myself by getting a glass of water. The salty taste in my mouth was disgusting. "It's a long story."

He followed me closely, without allowing me much personal space, which should have felt creepy, but didn't at all. "I think we've got time."

As if on cue, the lights he'd turned on when we'd stepped foot in the place, flickered and died and the wind shook the house violently. I dropped the glass I'd just taken out of the cupboard and yelped as it hit the ground next to my feet and shattered.

"Don't move." Roman's deep, authoritative command froze me in my tracks until I felt his warm hands grasp my waist.

I squirmed. "What are you doing?"

A rhetorical question. I knew what he was attempting to do. He was actually going to try to pick me up, obviously either overestimating his own abilities or he had no idea how much I weighed. He must not have gotten a good look at me. I was no lightweight, and I was horrified at the idea of him hurting himself by trying to lift me. I pushed at his hands to remove them, but they stayed firmly clasped.

"Stop, before you cut yourself." His voice was stern, and I found myself heeding his command. With seemingly no effort, as though I was a child, he hoisted me in the air and sat me down on the counter behind him. "Where do you think Greg or his wife might keep their broom?"

I sat there, in shock. The guy, Roman he'd said his name was, was big—far bigger than I was—but what he'd done by lifting me without effort shouldn't have been possible. He hadn't even grunted from the strain—nothing. "Uh, the Greg I knew wouldn't own a broom."

Roman chuckled and rested his hand on my knee. "Don't move. There's glass all over."

"What about your feet?"

"I'm tough."

Well, that was proving to be an understatement. I tried to follow Roman's movements through the darkness, perplexed. He'd lifted me like I weighed nothing. He'd swam with me on his back through turbulent waters and torrential rain. Who the hell was this guy? Superman? My heart raced. A wacky idea formed in my mind that maybe I was dead and dreaming. That had to be the case. None of this could be real. I slid off the counter and gasped when pain shot up my leg. Nope, not dreaming.

"What are you doing? I told you to stay up there." Roman was back, his hands on my waist again. Effortlessly, he lifted me back on the counter a second time, tsk-ing like I was an insolent child. This time, he spun me to the right until my foot rested against cold metal. The sink.

I gritted my teeth against the pain that had just started to register. His hands were warm as he held my calf, and I focused on that instead. "This is surreal."

He was close enough that I could feel his breath against my temple as he spoke. "What?"

I laughed. The laugh felt strange forming in my stomach, coming up my throat, tickling my lips. I couldn't remember the last time I'd laughed. "I almost died. I was trying to get out of the floodwaters and back to my house when the rip current caught me. Before I knew it, I was swept out to sea. Yet my worst injury of the day is from stepping on a piece of broken glass."

"Why do I feel like there's more to that story?" His hands were still on my leg. Was he aware that he was absently stroking my calf?

I blew out a frustrated breath at the reminder of my story. "In high school, Greg's parents kept the liquor in the cabinet above the fridge." I motioned with my head to the refrigerator behind me.

"Why don't you check? Maybe we'll get lucky. I think I need some. A lot."

Roman squeezed my thigh. "I can take a hint."

I found myself holding my breath. My heart was racing and there were butterflies in my stomach. I chalked them up to nerves from the storm and from almost dying, but part of me insisted they were from Roman's touch. Either way, I hoped the liquor would help settle them.

Roman pressed a bottle into my hand a second later. "Have at it while I clean up the glass. It'll help dull the pain when I clean up your foot in a minute. And do not get off that counter!"

I twisted off the lid and took a long pull from a bottle that turned out to be cheap vodka. I coughed and sputtered, but forced myself to swallow. A few more healthy swigs and the stuff didn't taste half bad. Before I got drunk, though, I put the lid back on and rested my head on my bent knee.

Roman came back with a lit candle and placed it on the other side of the counter facing me. It was then that I noticed the towel wrapped around his waist. I blinked a few times and replayed the last several minutes in my head. He hadn't been wearing a shirt. That, I remembered. But he'd had pants on. Hadn't he? Shorts, swim trunks, anything? The harder I tried to remember, the more I felt my face heat. He had been full monty and I hadn't even noticed. I guessed that the near-drowning experience affected me more than I'd first realized.

"Okay, let me look at your foot." He was gentle as he cupped my heel and lifted my foot from the sink.

I couldn't stop thinking about the fact that he hadn't been wearing anything. How had I not noticed? As my brain strained to fill in the gaps, against my better judgment, I barely noticed as he prodded my foot.

"This isn't going to feel good." He looked up. "I'm sorry, Megan."

I opened my mouth to ask why he was apologizing, or maybe why he hadn't been wearing clothes, but before the words emerged, a sharp pain ripped up my leg as he pulled a shard of glass out of my foot. At least, that was what I assumed he'd done. I screamed, unprepared for it.

Roman pressed a towel to my foot, but still managed to move close enough to wrap an arm around my shoulders and pull me against his chest in a hug. "I'm sorry. I know that hurt."

I shouldn't have turned my face into him. Or inhaled his warm, masculine aroma. He was a stranger and, despite my current marital situation, I did still have a husband. I kind of couldn't help myself, though. I was too shaken from—just everything—to fight the comfort his embrace brought.

"It's okay. We'll get some more cheap vodka into you and it won't hurt for much longer." His voice was so sure and strong. "I'll get you all fixed up. I promise I'll take care of you."

Those words spoken with such soothing reassurance nearly brought tears to my eyes. After the way I'd been treated by Dylan for the past few days, and far longer than that if I was being honest, having someone—even a complete stranger—say those words to me, "I promise I'll take care of you," and say them with genuine compassion and concern was like a drug to my soul. My heart skipped a beat and butterflies started up in my stomach. But, the side of my face was pressed against the bare chest of a man who wasn't my husband. I needed to stop. It wasn't a dream. It was reality, and the reality was that I was still a married woman.

I forced myself to pull away and blinked back an unexpected wave of emotion. "Um… I wonder if there's a working phone here. I should probably try to call my husband."

Roman visibly tensed and, a heartbeat later, moved away, clearing his throat. "I'll take a look around the place after I bandage your foot."

"Great, thanks." Why did his reaction make me want to crawl back into the ocean and let the storm carry me away?

9

ROMAN

Husband. My bear growled and thrashed as I focused on Megan's foot. A big piece of glass had sliced deep enough that she probably could've used stitches. As it was, several butterfly bandages would have to do. I shut my mind down and focused on the mechanics of the task as I cleaned her wound and dried it off. It was a challenge to focus with her sweet aroma and delicious curves enticing me. I got the smaller bandages on and then wrapped her foot in some gauze and taped it into place.

"There you go." I put some distance between us and focused instead on cleaning up the blood and wrappers from the bandages. "Be careful getting down, but you should sit on the couch and prop it up."

She cleared her throat. "Thanks."

I was tense as she lowered herself from the counter, waiting to catch her if she fell or screamed in pain again. A shiver went down my spine at the reminder of the pain I'd caused her when I'd removed the glass shard. The scream had been like a punch to the gut. Almost as bad as hearing her say she had a husband.

I couldn't help but watch her move away. She was tall for a human female, and her body was thicker than most of the women around the small island. Her hips were wide, her curves soft. I loved the look of her, especially the swell of her ass under the drenched T-shirt. It was as enticing, as the view of her from the front. Before the mention of a husband, I'd been dreaming of running my hands over those curves.

I swore softly and made myself look away. She was taken. She'd made a point of letting me know, too. She'd practically waved a big red flag in my face. It was perplexing, though. Because of the way I was reacting to her, my attraction to her that bordered on a soul connection, I would have guessed that she was my…

"I'm going to get cleaned up in the bathroom. I'm sure Greg, or his wife, has something I could wear for the time being." She limped toward the bedroom as my eyes followed. It made no sense. I let my head fall back and stared up at the ceiling. The way she called out to my bear, to me, was baffling.

I had to check in with the team.

Everything's good here. Local woman got sucked out to sea. Rescue was successful. We've taken shelter in a home on the beach. It's holding up well against the storm.

Serge's voice came back at me right away. *It took you fucking long enough. Did you have to swim to Siberia to pull her from the sea?*

No, asshole, I was administering first aid. She was unconscious and underwater when I reached her. And I'd been busy touching her and ogling her figure. *We'll wait out the storm here. Yell if you need anything.*

I looked around the house. Megan took the candle, but I didn't need it to see. My bear felt like he was ready to crawl out of my skin, the scent of Megan was driving him insane.

While waiting for her to return, I planted myself on the couch and listened to the battering rain of the storm raging outside. The house rocked ever so slightly, just enough to keep me on edge. Still, it was oddly cozy inside the house. And rather quiet. Too quiet. I was hyper-aware of every sound coming from the bedroom where Megan had gone.

The steady stream of swearing she was doing would've been enough to shock any sailor. I found myself grinning, listening to her.

"You okay in there?"

"Just peachy."

"You never told me the rest of your story. The long version."

She hesitated for a few moments. "I got swept out to sea during a hurricane. The end."

"There's definitely more to the story than that."

"My car probably got swept out to sea, too."

"Okay, how about all the in-between stuff you're leaving out?"

"I'd just put a few thousand dollars' worth of professional photographs in the back of it to keep them safe from the storm." She grunted. "Lot of good that did."

I whistled. "Why didn't you evacuate?"

Silence. After a while, I figured out she wasn't going to answer me, which made me want to know even more. I resolved to get the whole truth out of her. We had time. The storm wasn't going to let up for hours.

Settling back into the couch, I made myself as comfortable as I could with an angry bear pacing and clawing at my insides. Neither of us was pleased that Megan had a husband. My bear wanted me to go into the other room to be near her, to rub up against her and show her that we wanted her. I gritted my teeth against the urge and rested my forehead in my hand. Never before had I ever felt such a pull to be glued to a woman's side, but I drew the line at attempting to seduce a married woman.

"How long do you think the storm will last?" Her voice was soft as she called from the bedroom.

"It will be several more hours, at least, before it begins to let up. It's supposed to stall over us before moving farther north."

She sighed. "I hope the rest of my worldly possessions make it."

"Besides your car?"

"Besides my car. My house and my business. I didn't get to finish closing them up—not as securely as I would have liked." My guess was that revelation was the beginning of the rest of her story I was waiting to hear.

"No?"

"I found some clothes. I'll be out in a minute."

I heard the bedroom door shut and listened for the sound of a lock turning. *Good, lock me out.* I needed more signs that she wasn't mine. My bear wasn't accepting it, and I was having a hell of a time myself.

10

MEGAN

I stared at myself in the bathroom mirror. The candle Roman had procured was burning brightly, emitting a lavender aroma that was doing nothing to comfort me. I looked like a drowned rat. A giant rat, but still a rat. My hair was in sopping, frizzy curls that stood out in every direction like a perfect rat's nest. I still had slight traces of makeup from two days before, just a bit of mascara flakes and smears hanging out under my eyes. I had bags big enough to fit a couple of designer dogs in. The oversized white shirt I'd been wearing had turned into a see-through dress that was so heavy and cold that even wearing some of Greg's dirty laundry would've been an improvement.

Fortunately, I didn't have to resort to that. I got cleaned up the best I could and, rifling through Greg's dresser, found a pair of boxer shorts and a T-shirt. The shirt wasn't as loose as I would've liked. Greg was a thin guy, like Dylan. Dylan. My husband. Who was not the man on the forefront of my mind. It was the complete stranger in the next room that had monopolized my thoughts and had my mind spinning in circles.

Not just my mind, either. Butterflies seemed to have permanently housed themselves in my stomach. I was facing my reflection in the mirror, obsessing about how I looked and nervous about going back out to the living room with him. I was behaving like a schoolgirl and it was ridiculous. I kept telling myself to knock it off. It was inappropriate. I'd never seen the guy before in my life, and for all I knew, he could be a serial killer. He was probably out there sharpening his knife, getting ready to filet me.

Still, I was concerned about my ratty hair.

"You okay in there? How's the foot?"

I jumped as Roman's voice sounded from right outside the bedroom door. My hands shook slightly, but I forced myself to look away from the mirror and walk over to the door. "Yeah, I'm done."

Sure enough, he was standing just outside the door, and when I opened it, his eyes trailed over me. They stopped at my rat's nest and a smile stretched over lips. "Cute hair."

I ducked my head and limped around him. "I'm just going to prop my foot up."

"You do that. I'll bring you the vodka."

I didn't need vodka. I hadn't had a thing to eat and the last thing I wanted was to get shit-faced with a handsome stranger while huddled together in a beach bungalow as we weathered a tropical storm together. If that wasn't the perfect setting for a romance novel, I didn't know what was. Besides, I had a feeling I couldn't trust myself not to say or do anything stupid around Roman, especially if I was drunk.

He was some kind of magic man, though. When he stepped into the living room, he had the bottle of vodka in one hand, but he also had a bag of chips in the other—family size. The chips were exactly what I needed. He raised his eyebrows when my stomach growled and tossed them onto the couch beside me. "When's the last time you ate?"

I ripped into the bag and shoved a handful into my mouth, suddenly ravenous. "I don't even know. A day or two."

"What?" His scowl of disapproval spoke volumes.

I didn't need his approval, I told myself. I just needed food.

"What's the story, Megan? Are you in danger?" Right on cue, his eyes traveled to my upper arm. When I followed his gaze, I saw the fingertip bruises from Dylan. The longer sleeves on my T-shirt had covered them. Greg's didn't. "Who…"

I shouldn't have been so gratified to see the fury on Roman's face. I didn't know him. Yet, I felt warmed by the angry expression he wore on my behalf.

"Your husband?" His voice sounded a lot like a growl.

"It's not what it looks like." I took the bottle of vodka and downed a swig. "We own a business together and we were arguing… I bruise easily."

"What's his name?"

"Dylan. Dylan Pratt. We own Pratt's Photography on the north side of Main Street."

Roman's eyebrows raised. "I know the place. I walked by a few days ago. I'm guessing it was your husband I saw there. Why didn't he close up the place properly?"

I opened my mouth to lie for Dylan, as I'd done hundreds of times, then stopped. Roman didn't know us. I had no reason to lie to him, and maybe I was just sick of making excuses. "He refused. He doesn't do manual labor. He leaves it to me. I have a bigger build than he does, so he figures it's easier for me."

Roman's eyes looked like they were going to pop out of his skull. He snatched the vodka from my hand angrily and took a long pull himself before nodding to himself like he was making sense of things. "He told you that, did he? That you're bigger than him, so it's easier for you?"

Mortified, I scoffed. "No! No, that's not what I meant." And there I went making excuses again. "It's just, well, I *am* bigger. And stronger, so I do that stuff. He hates physical labor so he handles the office work."

Roman muttered something under his breath. I couldn't quite hear what he said, but it sounded an awful lot like he was calling Dylan a pussy.

Roman focused smoldering eyes on me. "You're not bigger or stronger than I am." Those seven words spoken aloud raised my core temperature to sizzling. The corner of his mouth twitched. "Are you?"

I couldn't look away from him. I needed to look away. Wild, frizzy curls, chip crumbs on my fingertips, vodka on my breath, I was a mess and I knew it. *Look away, Megan.* My eyes didn't cooperate. My voice was barely a whisper. "No, I'm not."

Finally, he shrugged and turned to set the vodka bottle down. Spell broken. Clearing his throat, he ran his hands down his face. The hint of stubble matched the golden blonde of his buzzed hair. "No, you're not."

I swallowed audibly and shoved more chips into my mouth. I had to get away from him. He was doing something to me that made no sense. Maybe I was ovulating or something.

"So, where is your small husband?"

Suddenly, the house shook with a hard wind gust, and I dropped the bag of chips and held onto the couch with both hands, chip crumbs and all. "Are we safe here?"

"I won't let anything happen to you. You're safe."

Why his words relaxed me, I didn't know. A man—even a buff, muscled one like him—who could confidently say he was no match for a hurricane was a little over the top egowise. Deciding it was time to step away from the chips, I glanced down at Greg's couch, covered in greasy crumbs, and winced. "I'll have to pay to have his couch cleaned."

"I doubt they'll notice your crumbs over the animal print."

I reached for the vodka bottle and took another pull. Roman had asked me a question and I could tell from the intensity of his gaze that he wasn't going to just let it drop unanswered. "Dylan evacuated in time. He's inland, somewhere."

Roman's jaw dropped. "He left you?"

I gave a tight little laugh. "Yeah, you could say that. In more ways than one."

"What kind of man leaves his wife to fend for herself in a hurricane?!" Roman began pacing the floor, fists clenching and unclenching at his sides. He looked like he was ready to go out and find Dylan just to beat the shit out of him. He shook his head at me.

"You almost drowned. You were underwater when I reached you, not breathing, seconds from the point of no return."

"Yeah, thank you for rescuing me, by the way." I leaned back into the couch, finding it incredibly comfortable. The vodka was hitting me a little harder than I'd meant it to. Still, I was sober enough to know that, now that I'd begun the story of why and how he found me in the water seconds from death, I had to say more. "Yeah, Dylan left. I had to close up the house and the shop myself. By the time I finished securing things, it was too late to get myself to safety."

"So, you tried to go home?"

I nodded. "And the east side of the island was already flooded. It's really my own fault. I should have known better. I should've boarded everything up days ago and given myself time to evacuate. I've never been this irresponsible before. It all just...snuck up on me."

"Dylan better hope Matilda carries *him* out to sea."

11

ROMAN

I was going insane. Megan had leaned over and was peacefully sleeping on the couch. It was as though she wasn't bothered at all by the story she'd just dropped at my feet. Her husband was a dick. Worse than a dick. A cowardly, sniveling, lowlife dick. Maybe it bothered me more than it should have, but I couldn't stop fuming. I wanted to rip out of my skin and find the motherfucker and maul him to shreds.

Her arm had nasty bruises from him. She'd nearly died alone because of him. I was going to make him pay for hurting her. He'd also pay for making her think it was her duty to assume a masculine role as though her size was a good excuse for him to not step up as a man. Her size was quite perfect in my opinion, and she was *all* woman.

I paced around the house, listening to the storm until I was ready to scratch my own eyeballs out. That way, I wouldn't have to be faced with the constant sight of Megan, the thin boxer shorts she wore riding up ever so slightly. Even those boxers were pissing me off. They belonged to Greg. Not me. I wanted to pull them off her and find something of mine to drape her in. Not his. Fuck Greg, the guy from high school. And fuck her dick of a husband—I wanted to rip that asshole to shreds.

The eye of the storm has arrived. It should be calm for about fifteen minutes. Want to make it here while you can? Serge sounded strained, even in my head. It was a tense situation not just for me, apparently.

Maybe. I'll let you know.

I was looking down at Megan. She was stunning. Even with her hair curling in every direction and potato chip crumbs dusting her mouth, she was beautiful. She deserved more than she was getting. I may not have known her well, but I knew that much. She was sweet and loyal, despite her husband not deserving her loyalty.

She groaned and grew restless. Her hands balled into fists on her lap. Her forehead scrunched, her expression was unhappy, and she pursed her lips. Dreaming of something unpleasant, she mumbled in her sleep and then grunted.

I didn't like seeing her unhappy, even in her sleep. It bothered me and it bothered my bear. I was already reaching for her when she mumbled her asshole husband's name and frowned even deeper. My bear growled and I squeezed my eyes shut, needing a second to get him under control, to get myself under control. I didn't know what it was about the woman that had me so agitated, but I was ready to tear up the place in anger over her mistreatment.

"Megan, wake up," I spoke her name gently, not wanting to scare her. Her eyes flew open, and when they focused on me, a light smile lifted her lips, and I fought an intense yearning, wanting so badly to draw her back against my chest that my arms ached.

Husband. What the fuck?

"The eye of the storm is coming. We can safely make it to my office, if you want."

She sat up and rubbed at her eyes. "I want to check on my house."

I nodded. "Okay."

"And the business."

"I don't know if we'll have time for both." I looked at my watch and thought about it. "Maybe, if we're fast and the water allows it. Otherwise, we'll get to your house and either bunk there or go on to my office. The rest of my team is there, waiting out the storm."

"Your team?"

I shrugged. "I work at the lifeguard station at the southern end of the island."

She nodded, like something made sense to her finally. "That's why you're so good at swimming. Okay. When do we go?"

For whatever reason, I felt uncomfortable lying to her. P.O.L.A.R. was a clandestine league, though. I didn't have the authority to reveal what we did or who we were just because I thought she was pretty and I was inexplicably attracted to her. "Soon. Does Greg or his wife have any shoes you can wear? Tennis shoes or something that lace up tightly?"

"I can look." She arched her back and reached her arms up in the air in a stretch. As she did, the hem of the shirt came up, revealing a sliver of stomach. I swallowed audibly, and she jerked it back in place and stood up. "Sorry."

I had more to say to her, more to ask her, but it wasn't the time. It'd never be the time for what I wanted to say. She was married. I kept my mouth shut and forced myself to look anywhere but at her.

When she returned a few minutes later, her limp was not as severe as before. "His shoe size is a 10. I don't think they'll fit you. And I'm pretty sure his clothes won't."

I looked down at the towel I was wearing and bit back a laugh. "I don't need shoes. Will they be too big for you?"

Her cheeks went so red I could see the blush even in the shadows of the house. "No. You should know I have big feet. You held my foot in your hand."

I frowned. "Size is relative. They aren't big to me."

She looked like she wanted to argue, but instead she just slid her feet into the shoes and laced them up tight. When she was finished, she stood up and looked around. "I'll leave a note for Greg. I'm sure he'll understand that we had no choice but to come in."

I didn't give a fuck about Greg. I didn't want to say that to her and make her think I was an asshole, though. *What's the word on the eye?*

You better hustle. Dmitry paused. *I suggest you avoid the office unless you want a giant fucking headache. Serge and Hannah are bickering because he won't stop freaking out about her safety. You're better off weathering Matilda head on.*

Copy that.

I went to the door and slowly opened it. Sure enough, it was eerily silent outside. No rain, no battering wind. I glanced up and found myself gazing up at a beautiful, starry sky. "We're in the eye. Come on."

"My house is on East Beach." Megan raced up behind me, looking over my shoulder to see what I was staring at. "Wow. That's so strange. But cool."

I didn't disagree. "Come on. We're going to have to swim. I'll go ahead to make sure there aren't rip currents."

"Wait, what if there are?" She grabbed my arm and shook her head. "Maybe we should just stay put. You don't have to do this for me. We can stay here and both be safe."

I looked down at her, the woman who thought she was big, and wanted to kiss her more than I'd ever wanted to do anything in my life. Was she worried about me? "There's no need to worry. I'm an incredibly strong swimmer and well trained. Lifeguard, remember?"

As she stared up at me, I watched her eyes travel to my mouth.

A gust of wind pushed at my back and I snapped back to reality. She cleared her throat and let go of my arm. "Just...be careful."

I wagged my eyebrows at her, wanting to relax her a bit. "We're in the eye of a hurricane, woman. Telling me to be careful is moot at this point."

She grinned at me, I saw just a flash of her true beauty, and then we were off.

12

MEGAN

Traveling in a hurricane was no fun. The trip to my house took so long that by the time we got to my porch, I felt like Matilda was right behind us, ready to strike up again any second. Sunkissed Key had already taken a beating, from what we'd seen, and she wasn't done. My house, fortunately, seemed to be okay. Some damage to the roof was evident, but it wasn't anything I wouldn't be able to fix myself.

As soon as we were in the house, I realized a few things right away. Every gust of wind sent the place rocking as though we were on a boat. More than that, I noticed what I'd somehow failed to notice that morning. Things were missing.

I went from room to room, checking for damage and creating a catalog of the missing items. When I got to the bedroom and looked into the closet, my stomach sank. Dylan's side was empty. All his clothes and shoes were gone.

I sat on the edge of my bed and stared at the empty half of the closet. When had he packed his stuff? How had I not noticed? I'd moved into the guestroom, but shouldn't I have noticed him packing and leaving with his things?

"Megan?"

I glanced up and found Roman staring at the half-empty closet, too. I sighed and tried to quickly bury the feelings that were threatening to surface. I wasn't even sure what they were, but I didn't want to have my emotions explode in front of Roman.

I stood up and wiped my hands on Greg's boxers, like that would wipe away the shock. "Everything seems in order here. Do you think we have time to get to the shop?"

He shook his head. "It's already starting up again."

I turned my back to the closet and nodded. "Okay. That's fine. I'm going to put on dry clothes and...I'll find something for you to wear, too."

Like magic, the towel had stayed around Roman's hips through the trip, but it was soaked and riding so low that I was getting a view of what I was pretty sure was the top of his "down there" hair. And those abs...whew. Danger zone. I turned to the closet and ran my hands through my hair.

"I'll find you something."

Roman chuckled from behind me. "I don't think you'll have anything big enough. Maybe another towel?"

I glanced back at him and shook my head. "I don't think I have towels big enough, either."

He flashed me a cheeky grin and wagged his brows again. "A sheet?"

I looked down at my bed and nodded. "Yeah, a sheet would probably do it. Okay, that'll work."

My door closed, and I glanced back to see he'd gone. In just the glow of a vanilla-scented candle, I stripped and changed into a T-shirt and a pair of yoga pants. I kept my back to Dylan's side as I flipped through clothes, searching for something for Roman.

The man was just...too big. He had to be close to seven feet tall and so broad chested that there was no way anything I had, even my bloat clothes meant for heavy-flow days, would fit him. I pulled an old baseball cap over my hair and went back into the bedroom.

The idea of giving Roman a sheet from our bed made me cringe. Dylan had slept with someone else on those sheets. Washed or not, I didn't want their filth anywhere near Roman. Instead, I went into the guestroom and took the flat sheet off the bed I'd been sleeping in. I told myself that it didn't mean anything, but the idea of a sheet that had touched my body wrapped around his bare skin sent a wicked shiver through me.

Downstairs, Roman was in the kitchen, staring into my darkened fridge. There was nothing in there. Nothing fresh anyway, but he'd managed to find a lone beer. The wet towel hanging around him was even lower and I could see the top of his ass.

"Sheet. I...I brought you a sheet." I turned away from the view and stammered. "It's from my bed."

The sound of the wet towel hitting the ground set my blood on fire. Roman was naked behind me and I could see him, in all his glory, if I just looked over my shoulder. I kept my eyes closed just in case I was tempted to try. He wasn't mine to look at. Why I was feeling so much like a hormonal teenager, I didn't know.

When we were leaving Greg's, I had this feeling that he was going to kiss me. And I wouldn't have minded. Thankfully he didn't actually try. Why I would have been willing to let him kiss me, I had no idea. I was married. Even if Dylan had left me.

That reality helped dampen my mood. My husband left me. He'd also taken things from around the house that weren't his. Artwork, every TV, the home desktop computer. When had he had time to take the TVs off the walls? It made no sense.

Again, I had more anger than sorrow. I had half a mind to find him and rip into him about what he'd done. Rip him apart—that's what I wanted to do if I was being honest with myself. I may have spent several days in denial, avoidance of the mess that was my marriage, but I was ready now to face the reality that my husband was a lying, cheating piece of crap who'd left me and I wanted to repay him for it. I also wanted to not give a shit about what my family would say and not give a shit about what it would feel like to be plunged into divorcehood.

"You want to talk about it?" Roman's deep voice was so close that I felt the vibrations in my chest.

He must have read my expression. I shook my head. I knew that if I opened my mouth, I was going to lose it. Whatever I was feeling was going to fire off like a missile and I didn't trust myself. I needed to think about everything a little more before I put any of my thoughts out into the world.

The house swayed harder and I gasped. "Greg's house didn't sway this much."

Roman put his hand on my shoulder and lightly squeezed, a comforting gesture, or it should've been. Instead, warmth radiated down my arm and chest in ways it had no business doing. "We're okay. Different construction, probably. It stood up to the first half of the storm, it'll stand up to the second half just as well."

Another powerful sway and I wasn't so sure.

"Come on. I found a beer. Drink it. It'll calm you while we ride out the storm on your couch. It's a lot prettier than Greg's animal print monstrosity."

I rounded the kitchen island and went straight to the liquor cabinet. Usually full for the parties that we didn't throw, I just stood there for a second, staring. It was empty. "He had time to pack the liquor."

Roman took my shoulders and gently turned me and pushed me away from the cabinet. "Take the beer."

13

ROMAN

If I expected myself to feel better seeing that Megan's husband had left her, I surprised myself. I was furious. How could he have done that to her? What the hell was wrong with the asshole? I wanted to hunt him down and demand that he beg for her forgiveness. She didn't deserve that type of treatment. I could see the emotion in her eyes, but she was bottling it inside.

I assumed she was heartbroken. No matter how she looked at me, and I was sure I saw heat in her gaze, to her I was some guy she'd just met. He was her husband. As much as it hurt to admit that, it was true. She'd married the asshole. That meant she loved him. She was hurting, and I didn't like it.

I led her to the living room and to the couch, sitting next to her, ready to be a shoulder for her to cry on. Handing her the beer, I bumped her shoulder with mine. "Talk."

Instead of crying, she started laughing. She popped right back off the couch and started pacing in front of me. The swaying of the house would throw her off a bit, here or there, but she was focused on wearing a hole through the rug.

"Sonofabitch. He took the liquor. Who does that? I mean, the TVs?

Okay, fine. He loves TV, so I get that, kind of. The liquor, though? He doesn't even drink the stuff. He likes wine. What the hell is that? Maybe *Brandi* likes liquor."

I just watched as she went on.

"We've been married for over ten years. This December would be twelve years, actually. Twelve years of marriage and he fucks someone named Brandi—in our bed!" She nodded to the sheet around my waist and crinkled her nose. "Not on that sheet. Don't worry. I gave you my bedding."

I knew that. It carried her scent so strongly that I had to mouth breathe to keep from getting aroused. "Thanks for that."

She paused. "And that. You say thank you. I can't remember the last time Dylan thanked me for anything. He just expects me to bend over backward for him, and the only time he acknowledges it is if I don't do it. Then, he has plenty to say."

"The shop? I do everything. It was my money that financed the business and I'm the photographer. I shoot the photos, edit them, do all the matting and framing myself, and I run the floor while he sits in the back office doing *the important part.* What important part? What else is there to do? I literally do everything, and when I finally get home, I have no time to do anything but eat and sleep. How did he have time to sleep around?"

"I think you answered that."

She stopped and made a face. 'True. I'm so angry. I want to rip his goddamn head off."

"I can arrange something like that."

"I caught them sleeping together, you know. I walked in on them. In our bed. He didn't even apologize. He just basically made me feel like I was at fault for not seeing it coming." She took off the baseball cap she'd been wearing and twisted her hair up on the top of her head. After securing it with some band she had on her wrist, she pressed her palms against her eye sockets. "He stole all the money from the shop. The shop that's probably getting torn apart right now because he took no responsibility for securing it against the storm. I tried to do it myself, but I'm only one person."

I remained calm on the outside, but her pain had me raging internally. My bear was ripping at me, desperate to get out and kill the stupid shit that would treat Megan so horribly.

"I can't believe he took the liquor. I mean, that's just low."

I opened the beer and handed it to her. "I can't believe he thought he could find someone better than you."

She stopped pacing and faced me. Then, she snorted a laugh through her nose as if in disbelief. "You don't have to say that. I know that I have flaws, too. Plenty of them. Just...not the ones *Brandi* has, apparently."

"I'm not telling you anything that isn't true. Even a stranger can see that you're loyal and kind, even to a man who doesn't deserve it. It's not hard to imagine how well you'd treat a good man. A better man." *A man like me.* I cocked my head and looked at her harder. "And that's saying nothing of your beauty."

"Which I lack." She shook her head, and the ball of hair on top of it wobbled. "I still deserve better, though."

"Worlds better. And your beauty is hardly lacking. Megan, you're gorgeous. I'm not going to make you uncomfortable by telling you just how attractive I find you, but I'm not exaggerating when I say I think your husband is the biggest fucking idiot on the planet."

Her cheeks were rosy, and she looked away before taking a long pull from the beer and then passing it back to me. Our fingers brushed when I took it, and I felt the connection down to my toes. Her slight gasp told me she felt it, too.

"Do you love him?"

"No." She covered her mouth with her hand, shocked that she'd answered so quickly, or maybe it was the answer itself that shocked her. "I mean...well...no. We've grown apart. Maybe I should've known something like this was coming. I can't remember the last time I felt a connection to him. More than that, I don't know if I even like him. But we made vows to each other. We promised..."

"You wish you could have remained with him?"

She met and held my gaze, pain and confusion evident in her eyes. She was clearly hurt by everything that was happening to her and felt she had little control. "I…don't know. No, I guess not. I guess I was living a fantasy. Pretending he was someone else, a different kind of man, and that *we* were something else. Before I was rudely shaken back to reality. I don't what to be with someone who could do this."

"Someone who could take the liquor?"

She laughed lightly and rolled her eyes before taking the beer bottle back from me. "Yeah, someone who could take the liquor."

I smiled at her and shrugged. "So, you don't love him and you don't want to be with him."

She shook her head. "I guess not, no. I'm thirty-two, though. I can't just start over. I don't want to be like the rest of my family going through marriages the way normal people go through mascara."

"Mascara?"

"Makeup. You're supposed to throw it away after six months. It's dangerous to use it… Not the point. The point is, I don't want to start over."

"So, you'd be happy if he returned?"

"No."

"I don't think you're making much sense right now."

She sank onto the couch next to me and turned her head so she was looking at me. "I want him to magically be someone else entirely." She let out a long, slow sigh. "I don't want to be alone."

I raised an eyebrow. "Let him go. I promise you won't be alone."

Megan's eyes rolled and she scoffed. "Yeah, okay."

I caught her chin in my hand and lifted her face so she was looking at me. She thought so little of herself. I didn't understand how it was possible. She was beautiful, and sexy. To me she was more beautiful than any woman I'd ever seen before. My heart raced when I looked at her, and I desperately had to be closer to her. I wanted her. As I thought it, I realized that I wanted more than be closer to her. I wanted every part of her. I wanted her to have every part of me.

Megan blinked and bit her lip. "Why are you looking at me like that?"

There was no more denying it. This woman was my mate. My stomach tightened and my bear roared, confirming my suspicion.

She was the one—ours. Before I had time to consider the revelation more fully, Maxim's voice broke through my thoughts.

Tornado incoming, brother.

14

MEGAN

My entire body was tense. Roman was staring at me like he wanted to kiss me again, and damned if I didn't want him to. I had no business wanting him the way I did, but I couldn't stop the feeling.

"Fuck." Roman was on his feet in a split second and had me up and in his arms just as fast. "Tornado."

I was still in romantic la-la land. "What?"

He picked me up in a bear hug and literally ran us toward the bathroom. "Tornado."

The word clicked into place in my brain just as the house swayed harder and a sickening howl sounded. "Oh, fuck."

Roman shoved me into the bathroom and vanished, only to reappear a few seconds later with half the couch cushions in his arms. "In the tub. Get in the tub, Megan!"

I no sooner did as he said, then he was on top of me, the cushions on top of him. Flattened on the bottom of the tub, the weight of Roman plastered to me, I felt fear for all of two seconds before my body switched back into hormonal-teenager mode. A tangle of limbs and cushions, Roman was twisted to fit over me, but our faces had somehow ended up inches apart.

I could hear a shutter come loose upstairs. The banging that followed probably should've worried me more. The house was being damaged. With Roman on top of me, though, his face was hovering just above mine, his breath mingling with mine, and his bedroom eyes focused on me, I kind of didn't care about anything else.

"Am I too heavy?"

I shook my head the slightest bit. "Nope."

His arms were planted on either side of my head and he shifted slightly. "I don't believe you."

"I like it." I realized what I'd said and stuttered. "I mean, it's, um, fine—nice. Like a weighted blanket."

"You like it?" His breathing shallowed and his eyes flicked down to my lips.

I told myself to change the subject or to say no. I couldn't, though. I just watched him. I looked at his mouth, the fuller top lip enticing, then at his eyes. Those thick lashes lowered. "Yes."

"Megan?" He looked down at my mouth again, and the gap between us became even smaller.

"Yes." I didn't even know the question, but my answer was still yes. I felt like my blood was on fire. I could feel him pressed against me and I wanted more. My body had woken up for what felt like the first time.

Roman's lips were a breath away from mine, and I felt pulled into his magnetic field. His lips rested against mine, and I felt him shudder before pulling back just enough to speak. "I'm going to kiss you."

He already had, but I didn't argue. I nodded, bumping our noses together. "Yes."

He kissed me again, and I realized that he meant he was *really* going to kiss me that time. His mouth was warm and passionate against mine, his beard rough against my skin. His forearm wedged between my head and the tub to provide support and then he licked the seam of my lips, demanding entrance.

"Yes." I gripped his sides, the only thing my hands could reach, and held on while he stroked his tongue over my lips. Electric currents had nothing on his kisses.

Pulling back and then kissing just my bottom lip, his mouth made love to mine. When his tongue slipped into my mouth, it tangled seductively with mine. His fingers pressed into my scalp and I could tell he wanted more. Unable to be still, I tried to maneuver so I could feel more of his body pressed against mine. I got one leg free and twisted my hips just the right way. Roman's body lined up with mine just right, and I could feel his hard length pressing between my thighs.

I cursed my yoga pants and wrapped my leg around his hip. Stroking his tongue back and then sucking his top lip, I heard myself moan, but couldn't care. Roman deserved to know what he was doing to me. His other hand worked down and gripped my ass, pulling into his body.

Tired of being confined, Roman sat up, knocking the cushions all around. Still kissing me, he pulled me to my feet and then into his arms. Locking my legs around his waist, I moaned into his mouth at the feeling of his body between my legs.

The sounds of the storm raged on outside of the bathroom, but it didn't faze us. I felt the counter under my ass and then Roman's hands under my shirt, stroking the skin of my back. I ran my hands over his skin, finding ridges and dips of muscles. He was smooth and soft, the light dusting of hair rougher. I opened my legs wider and cursed the sheet between us.

Roman tugged at the hem of my shirt. Up and off, it was lost to the darkness of the bathroom. He slid his hands into my leggings and growled.

"Too fast?" His voice was like gravel. It shook with an audible need.

I shook my head and ran my hand down his arm. Catching his hand, I delighted at the size of it before pulling it out of my leggings. I lifted myself and pushed them down. Roman caught them and yanked them the rest of the way.

I tried to pull him back between my thighs, but he resisted. "Roman?"

He kissed me. "Let me taste you. Please."

I hesitated. "What?"

His hand stroked up my bare thigh and then cupped my sex. "I need to taste you. Here. I need you in my mouth, Megan."

I swallowed. That was...a lot. Dylan didn't do that. It'd been...years.

"Say yes." He kissed me and then went down to his knees. Kissing my inner knee, then my inner thigh, he moaned. "Fuck, Megan, say yes for me."

"Yes."

He growled and raked his teeth over my thigh. "You're stunning. I want to taste and lick every part of you."

I gripped the edge of the sink as he pulled me forward. His face was right in front of my sex, and I was torn between wanting him to do it and wanting to cover myself and run out of the room to avoid having him see me. What the hell was wrong with me? Dylan had really made me that insecure about my sexuality?

His tongue stroked my inner thigh and then he nipped me there. When I jerked, he growled and pulled my thighs onto his shoulders.

I tried to hold myself off him, knowing I was heavy.

He just pulled me farther so I had no choice. Resting my weight on his shoulders, I gripped the countertop and let my head fall back. Roman made a delighted moan and nipped closer to my sex. "That's it. I want all of you."

I squirmed at the first flick of his tongue across my folds. The second went deeper and I gasped. When he stroked his tongue deeper, I clamped my teeth down over my lip to keep the sounds from escaping.

"Let me hear you. I want to know what I do to you, Megan. I want to hear you." When Roman stroked his tongue over my most sensitive spot, I squeaked. That made him growl against it and flick his tongue harder.

Helpless to his assault, I panted, I moaned, I cried out. He rewarded me with harder and faster flicks of his tongue and then by sucking me into his mouth. Where had he read the book on exactly what my body liked? Within seconds, I was on the edge, fighting to keep an orgasm at bay. Roman would have none of it, though. He licked and sucked me right over that edge and kept going.

15

ROMAN

My mate. I knew for sure now. I didn't want our first intimate encounter to have any negative feelings attached for her, so I didn't go past tasting her. When I finally finished and she'd come on my tongue a few more times, I pulled her shirt back over her head and helped her get her pants back on. She was quiet as I dressed her and then settled us back in the tub with her curled between my legs, the sheet back in place.

I was rock hard and desperate to take her and mark her as mine, but I knew that she had unfinished business to attend to first. But she was going to be mine and that was that. I wasn't going to share her with anyone once I marked her. Already, the possessiveness I felt over her was overwhelming.

"I can do that for you, too…" Her voice was quiet, shy.

I tilted her head up to look at me and found that she wouldn't meet my eyes. Growling lightly, I nipped at her shoulder through her shirt. "Don't clam up on me."

Meeting my heated gaze, she lifted her chin and licked her lips. "I can return the favor. I'm not… I'm not greedy. I don't want to be greedy, I mean."

My dick throbbed, but I ignored it. "I'd love that, but another time.

That was about you. About me showing you what I think of you. How attractive and sexy and magnetic I find you."

She didn't breathe. "Later?"

I leaned forward and caught her mouth in a kiss. "Later."

Heat burned in her eyes, but she just nodded and settled against my chest again. "Later."

I wrapped my arms around her waist and sighed, content with where I was. For the first time since landing in Florida, I wasn't focused on the stifling heat, or the fact that I missed the steady action of our missions in Siberia. I felt like I'd just come home and it was time to relax.

"I don't know anything about you." Her fingers stroked over my arms. "And, god, what does that say about me?"

I held her tighter. "It doesn't say anything about you, but that you want me and I want you."

"What about you, though?"

"What about me?"

"Tell me something about yourself. You've heard all about my recent melodrama. I wanna know about you."

I wrapped my legs around her as the storm raged on outside. Cradling her, ready to save her with my life, I pressed my lips against her hair. "My team and I moved here just a little while back. A month ago. We were in Siberia. Now, we're here."

"*Siberia?*"

"Yeah. We all grew up there."

"What? That's so unexpected. You sound like you could've grown up down the street." She rested her head on my shoulder and smiled. "What kind of lifeguarding does one do in Siberia?"

I chuckled. My mate was sharp. "The lifesaving kind. And where we grew up is kind of an area of expats. I can speak perfect Russian for you, if you'd like.

I dropped my voice and spoke to her in my native tongue. "вы прекрасны."

She giggled. "I like it."

"I like you."

"No, we're talking about you. Tell me more."

"What do you want to know?"

With a little shrug, she sighed. "I don't know. Have you ever been married?"

"No."

"Girlfriend?"

"Of course not."

"Children?"

"No. Do you have children?"

"No. I would've mentioned them by now." She looked up at me. "What's your favorite food?"

"All of it." I smiled. "Do you cook?"

Megan nodded. "I'm a good cook. I learned from my nana growing up. She was a stereotypical Italian grandmother who lived to feed her family homemade meals. She taught me everything."

"I can make sandwiches."

"That's not cooking."

"Well, it's better than most of the guys on the team can do. That's got to count for something."

"Are your parents still living?"

"Yes. They're still together, living happily in Siberia." I smiled to myself. "They still act like kids."

"That must've been nice growing up."

"It was. How was your life growing up?"

Her hands went still and she curled into herself more. "Fine, I guess. We had money and I never wanted for anything."

"But?"

"But my parents were only married for three years, and I don't even know how many stepsiblings I have. I have several half-siblings that I don't see. Typical rich-kid sob story. My nanny raised me. Mommy and Daddy didn't spend enough time with me. Blah, blah, blah."

"We don't have those stories where I come from. You'll have to tell it to me some time."

With a light laugh, she began stroking my arms again and settled back into me. "Are you really this nice?"

I frowned. "I guess?"

"You don't know?"

"I'm not sure what you mean. I haven't really done anything especially nice."

She sat up and turned to face me. I missed her in my arms instantly. "You saved my life. You are very kind and generous in the things you say and the way you say them. You did...that...*you know* to me without demanding anything in return. You're nice."

I scowled. "Wow, your standards are low. I saved you because you needed help and it's what I do. The things I say are completely true. And what I did to you was just as much for me as it was for you. I wanted the taste of you on my lips."

She blushed and turned back into me. "Okay."

"You deserve more than what he has given you." I pulled her back against my chest and breathed in the scent of her hair. "I can show you."

She stayed quiet. If she thought for a minute I just meant sexually, though, she had another thing coming. I didn't care if I ever went back to Siberia anymore. She was my mate, and she was going to learn through my actions what to expect from a mate. I was going to make sure she knew how she deserved to be treated. And what *nice* really meant.

16

MEGAN

Spending the rest of the night in the tub with Roman should've been uncomfortable. Somehow, I'd dozed against his chest and got the best sleep I could remember having in years. When I came awake the next morning, I was still in his arms and he was stroking my hair. I didn't want to read too much into it. What would a man like Roman see in a woman like me? The whole night was probably just a coping mechanism—human contact as a way to deal with an intense situation. Yet, the way he looked at me promised so much more. Or maybe I was being overly hopeful since I wanted more.

"Storm's over."

I climbed to my feet and smiled down at him. "I need to brush my teeth and then look around the house. You probably need to go check on your team."

Shaking his head, he stood up and out of the tub, right into my space. Cupping my face, he kissed me tenderly and grinned against my mouth. "Trying to get rid of me?"

Not a chance. I'd given up on ignoring the sexual attraction I felt when next to him. I wanted him to stay and keep doing really amazing things to me. "Nope."

"Good."

I found him a spare toothbrush and we brushed our teeth together, our eyes meeting in the mirror, a tense game of awareness. His chest was still bare and I could still feel his beard between my thighs. When we were finished and I put the toothpaste away, Roman picked me up and sat me on the counter, kissing me deeply. He gripped my ass and rocked his erection into me.

"Good morning."

I bit my lip when he pulled away and sighed. He was so hot. "Good morning."

"I need to get myself some clothes."

Did he really? I trailed my eyes over his back as he walked out of the bathroom and fought the urge to drag him back inside. "Okay."

"I'll be back in just a few minutes, okay? Stay here until I get back? We can go check on your shop together."

I arched an eyebrow and shrugged. "I guess."

He pulled me into his arms and nipped my lip. "Please?"

Melting against him, I nodded.

Laughing, he backed away. "I'll be back as fast as I can."

I didn't want to see him leave, for some reason, so I climbed the stairs to investigate the crash I'd heard the night before. I wondered how much damage had been done.

I had to laugh. The master bedroom window had shattered. It'd rained into the room and the bed was soaked—ruined, without a doubt. Nothing else was severely damaged inside the house. I'd gotten lucky.

I took a fast shower and got dressed in another pair of yoga pants and a T-shirt. By the time I got back downstairs, Roman had returned. Seeing him standing in the doorway, in a pair of board shorts and a T-shirt, I realized I'd missed him. I was happy to see him back, and something inside of me breathed a sigh of relief. It should've scared me that I was getting attached to a man so far out of my league. And, even though my husband left me for another woman, I was technically still married. It was a recipe for disaster, but when he smiled at me, I felt like he'd missed me, too.

I stepped into his open embrace and wrapped my arms around his waist. He smelled like cedar and citrus and was so warm. I wanted to stay curled in his arms all day. "Hi."

He wagged his brows at me. "You look beautiful."

I looked down at my bare feet and ignored the compliment. "How is it out there?"

"Rough." He took my hand and led the way out to the porch. Part of it was missing. "It looks like the porch and the upstairs window are the only things that suffered significant damage. A few shingles on the roof, but I can fix that easily."

I grinned. "I can, too."

"Touché."

The water had receded and left behind seaweed and lots of debris. The streets were littered with bricks and boards and bits from damaged homes—and probably my porch. Most of the houses I could see weren't damaged beyond repair, though. With some hard, steady work, we could get the island back in good shape in a month or so.

"You stayed behind, Megan?!" My neighbor, Cameron Patrick, stood in her driveway with her hands on her hips. "I thought you left with Dylan. I saw him loading stuff up in his sports car."

I dropped Roman's hand, instantly ashamed of myself. I'd forgotten that I was on the island that Dylan and I had made our home. People knew we were married. I couldn't be out with Roman as though it was completely normal. I winced and rubbed at my head, a headache forming already.

"You okay, honey?"

I blinked a few times and then nodded at Cameron. "Sorry, yeah. I was just… The storm really freaked me out. I usually evac, but I got caught up in it. Did you stay?"

"No way. Bobby and I left days ago. We had a little vacation at his mom's. I had to come back first thing this morning, though. You know how I love this little house."

I looked over her house and forced a smile. "Looks like you faired pretty well."

"Yeah, we did." As her gaze fell on Roman, she looked like she was about to jump out of her skin. "Who's your friend, honey?"

Roman stepped forward and shook her hand. "Roman. I'm newer to the island. Megan and I ended up stranded together last night."

Cameron sighed happily. "How romantic."

I blushed and didn't know what to say, so I just stared at her.

She rolled her eyes and waved me off. "You deserve a night of being stranded with a man like Roman, honey. Dylan mentioned to Bobby that you caught him cheating last week. I didn't know about any of it, I swear. I'm still mad at Bobby for not telling me. I would have come to you immediately. Before you had to find out like you did, I mean."

I had no words, so I just nodded.

Thankfully, Roman was there to save me again. "Well, it was nice meeting you, but we've got to run."

He didn't take my hand for the rest of the walk to the shop. He just walked by my side and shared the silence with me. I was floored to know that my neighbors knew about Dylan cheating on me. If Bobby Patrick knew, everyone knew. I was a joke. The laughingstock of the neighborhood. Not that I had a right to feel self-righteous or anything. Not after what I'd done with Roman. I didn't feel like I had much of a leg to stand on.

When we got to the shop, I just stood there in complete shock. Where the building used to be, there was now only a frame of a building. The whole place had been wiped out—reduced to a pile of rubble.

I waited for tears or even sorrow to hit, but I just kept staring, feeling more and more relieved as the minutes passed. Then, I laughed. The whole damn shop was gone. Matilda had wiped me clean out of the business I shared with Dylan. I still had my house, but my SUV was gone, the shop was gone, and my husband was gone. It was like fate had snipped all of the ties I had with the life I was living a week ago.

"You okay?"

I wiped my eyes, tears forming from laughing, and then took Roman's hand. "Yeah. I'm...uh...I'm good, actually. Really good."

17

ROMAN

I didn't know what was going on inside of Megan's head, but she'd taken my hand again. When her fingers intertwined with mine, I felt like the luckiest guy on the island. She'd just found her business destroyed, yet she was laughing. Why was she happy? I didn't want to chance upsetting her, so I just walked with her. To the other end of town we went, taking in the extent of the damage along the way.

I was sweating, but I felt like the heat wasn't as miserable with Megan next to me. I couldn't focus on it as much when she was there. "Want to meet my team?"

She nodded. "I'd like that. Your lifeguarding team from Siberia."

I nodded. It was obvious she didn't buy the lifeguarding story, but she didn't push either. She just accepted it.

The P.O.L.A.R. office was standing unharmed. There didn't appear to be any damage done to it at all. The door was wide open and gripes and complaints could be heard coming from inside. With the power out, there was no AC. The rest of the guys were probably roasting.

"I'm coming in with a guest. Are you all decent?"

Serge came to the door and grunted. "Are they ever?"

"Serge, this is Megan. Megan, my alph—*boss*, Serge." I kept my hand on her back, my bear was bristling, not at all appreciating that I was leading her into an office full of other unmated males.

Hannah stepped out from under Serge's arm and smiled at Megan. "Another woman. Thank god."

I introduced everyone. Megan smiled politely and said hello to everyone, but she remained close to my side, her back pressed against my hand harder, like she needed the connection, too.

"The generator isn't working. I can't take this torture." Alexei wiped his face and growled. "A couple more degrees and I'm going to spontaneously combust."

Megan snorted but tried to hide it behind a cough. "Sorry. I could take a look at it. I'm good at fixing things."

Serge raised his brows. "Yeah, sure. Have at it."

"If you fix it, I'm going to plant the biggest kiss on you, Megan." Alexei winked at her and blew her a kiss.

I surprised everyone by curling my lip, baring my teeth, and growling at him. Staring him down, I pulled Megan into my side and shook my head at him. "No."

Megan just giggled and pointed to the back of the building. "The generator around there?"

Serge nodded, his mouth slightly ajar. "Roman?"

"Later." I followed Megan like a lost bear cub, happy to trail behind her for the view, if nothing else.

"Did you just growl at your friend?" Megan found the generator on the ground by the back door and sank to her knees in front of it.

I didn't want to talk about it. I didn't want her to think I was scary. Or weird. She didn't know my nature. Until she did, she wouldn't understand. "How'd you learn to fix things?"

She looked back at me over her shoulder, those hazel eyes crinkled at the corners like she was enjoying herself. "Okay, we won't talk about how you growled like a zoo animal back there. I learned how to fix stuff by just doing it. When I first moved into my house, it was quite a fixer-upper. I watched hours and hours of YouTube videos. That got me pretty far. Trial and error took me the rest of the way."

I knelt beside her and watched as she did her thing. Without any tools, she was limited, but within five minutes, the generator roared to life. I laughed as a loud cheer rang out from inside. "Looks like you're the real hero here."

I loved the smile that spread across her face—and the confidence. "What can I say?"

Her genuine smile was so beautiful that my chest ached looking at her. "Should we head back to your house, now?" I had to admit, I had an ulterior motive for getting her alone again.

Her eyes went to my mouth and darkened. With a nod, she stood up and dusted off her hands on her pants. "Yeah, I guess I better get started with those repairs. The sooner the better."

"Stop by and see Susie, Roman. She was climbing the walls worried about you last night." Alexei stuck his head out of the back door and winked at Megan again. "And you, sweets, you're welcome to stay here. You miracle worker you."

I gritted my teeth and barely held my bear from bursting forth and attacking the hell out of Alexei. "Go!"

He just grinned cockily. He'd been intentionally trying to get my goat. "Don't forget Susie."

I sighed. I wanted nothing more than for the two of us to head straight back to Megan's, but Alexei was right. I should stop by Susie's. "Quick stop on the way?"

Megan nodded. "As long as you're talking about the Susie Davies at the Bayfront Diner, I'm more than happy to accompany you. Especially if her shop sustained little damage and she's back up and running. I could use a cinnamon roll."

When she grinned, I pulled her into me and kissed her, unable to stop myself. "I guess I should feed you."

"I think I can feed myself."

"We could feed each other?"

Blushing, she pulled away and looked out at the ocean. "It's crazy how much it can change so quickly."

"The ocean?" I watched the sea with her, my hands itching to touch her again.

"Life."

"My people put a lot of significance in change. We're always changing, shifting. Change is good."

When she looked back at me, she was blinking away tears. "Maybe you're right."

"Come here."

She wiped her eyes and let me pull her into my side. My need to claim her transformed into a need to take care of her, and I wanted to hold her until she realized how much good her change in marital status would bring both of us.

"I don't know what I'm doing, Roman."

I stroked her hair and pressed my lips to her forehead. I wanted her to be mine and all mine right this minute, to be as devoted to me from here on out as I was to her, but I couldn't expect that. She did have feelings for me, of that I was sure, but she probably couldn't comprehend why she was feeling them so intensely or so quickly. "I know. You'll catch up."

She looked up at me and her brows wrinkled. "There's something you're not telling me."

I stared into her eyes, desperate to lay all my cards on the table. Knowing the turmoil she'd been through in the past couple days, though, I wasn't sure she was in the right frame of mind to have another life-changing bomb dropped at her feet.

She wasn't ready to hear the whole fated-mates concept quite yet. "Not right now. Later."

She made a face. "It's always later with you."

"It'll be worth the wait."

She walked a few steps away and looked at me over her shoulder. "I'll be the judge of that."

18

MEGAN

Dropping in for breakfast at Susie's turned out to be an hours-long endeavor. As we strolled Main Street, we ended up stopping to help several different people along the way. Someone needed help removing a tree that had fallen across their driveway. Someone else needed help getting debris cleared away from the front door and into a pile. Roman was never reluctant to pitch in and lend a hand, even to perfect strangers—so different from Dylan. And he seemed to have the strength of ten men! They sure made them tough in Siberia. When people saw him coming, smiles lit their faces. He'd said he'd just arrived on the island a month before, but it was obvious that he'd made an impression in a month's time, and it was easy to see why. He was friendly and generous to everyone.

Dylan wasn't very friendly, and I'd never seen him be generous to anyone but himself. How had I been in denial about him for so long? No one smiled when he walked into a room or when he passed them in the street. No one was excited to see him. And it wasn't hard to figure out why. He either acted as though he was superior to people, or he outright ignored them. I'd even had customers complain about him to me, not knowing that he was my husband. And, of course, I'd made lame excuses for him.

My mind kept going in circles comparing Dylan to Roman, but there wasn't much time to dwell on the comparisons or formulate any conclusions. We stumbled into people that could use our help, and every time, Roman would shoot me a look as if to ask if I minded before he rushed to their aid. He was considerate and thoughtful, two things that I found so refreshing.

We worked until my body ached, and I wasn't sure I could propel myself up the stairs to my house, much less clear away another pile of rubble. Roman didn't seem to have the same problem. He was so strong that he made everything look easy. Next to him, I actually felt small and feminine for the first time in my life. I found myself thinking about what it would be like to slip on one of his T-shirts. It would be large on me, maybe even fit like a dress. I loved that thought.

As tired as I was, my libido still reacted when I looked at him, remembering the way his body felt against mine. But I was exhausted. My bones ached, and the lack of proper sleep, not just last night, but for the past week, was catching up to me.

I watched Roman, still hauling trash and piling it out of people's way. The man had probably cleared a quarter of the island himself. As if he sensed my gaze on him, he looked back at me. His gaze instantly turned heated. Self-consciously, I ran my hands over my hair and then crossed my arms over my chest. I was sweaty, dirty, and I knew my hair was a wreck.

"You are so beautiful." Roman straightened and walked over to me. Mr. Barnes was watching. His wife, Luanne was watching, too.

I forced a smile. "Yeah."

He caught my face in his hands and tipped my head up so I had to look him in the eyes. "I should've taken you straight back to your house this morning. I'm sorry."

Luanne smacked Mr. Barnes on the arm, and they both looked away from us. I knew my cheeks were red and I was so tired that tears filled my eyes. It was embarrassing.

Roman wrapped his arms around me and held me. "Tired?"

I nodded into his chest and sighed. "Sorry. It was a long night, I guess."

"I'll swing back by tomorrow morning to help, John." Roman scooped me into his arms and smiled down at me. "I have to get my girl home."

"Put me down, Roman. I'm too heavy." I squirmed. I wasn't about to let him carry me home. Besides the fact that I really was too heavy, people would see us.

"Do I look like I'm struggling?"

I stopped and looked up at him. He didn't. Not even an inkling of strain anywhere on his face. "What are you, Superman?"

He shot me a panty-melting grin and shrugged. "I'll tell you someday."

"This is insane. You're going to break your back."

"By carrying you? Hardly." He bounced me and laughed when I gasped and locked my arms around his neck. "I'm carrying you. Deal with it."

I stopped fighting since we were so close to my house. I figured he'd put me down when he needed to, and I might as well just enjoy it. His neck was damp under my hands and he was drenched in sweat, but instead of finding the smell of him a turn off, it had the exact opposite effect. He smelled warm and cedary and citrusy and I wanted to rub against him and trap that smell in my brain forever.

I remained in his arms as he carried me to my house, up the stairs, inside, and all the way to the guestroom. He dropped me on the bed and reached over his shoulder to grab his shirt and pull it over his head. In low-slung shorts and a whole lot of glistening abs, he looked down at me and licked his lips. "I'm hungry, Megan."

I stuttered. His smoldering facial expression had sent my brain out to the stratosphere, so his words caught me off guard. "I… I could fix something. There's probably something in the—"

He ran his hand up my calf and didn't stop until his fingers were playing with the hem of my leggings. "Not for that."

I stupidly giggled when I realized what he meant. My heart sped up and my body hummed. When he tugged at my yoga pants, I lifted my hips and let him pull them off of me. The mean little voice at the back of my head screamed that it wasn't a good idea to let him see me in that light. My thighs jiggled too much, my stomach was too soft, my hips too wide, my breasts too small. Not to mention I'd been sweating and I could use a shower.

Roman tossed my yoga pants across the room, pressed his lips to my ankle, and as though he'd read my mind, said, "You smell delicious. Absolutely delicious."

I rolled my eyes, despite my heart racing in my chest. "Sure."

He licked up to my calf. "Like sunshine and cool spring water. I want to devour you."

My mouth went dry. I shivered.

"Roman..." My voice was unrecognizable, breathy and full of desire. It was full-on sex kitten, come-hithering my man to me.

One knee on the bed, Roman moved closer to me.

"Megan? Are you here?"

Roman's head snapped up, the look in his eyes ferocious.

I jerked out of the bed, in a full-on panic, and grabbed for my yoga pants. "Oh, shit. Oh, no."

"Megan?!" My husband's voice called up the stairs, his footsteps following.

Roman pushed the door closed and looked back at me. "I wasn't finished."

I wanted to laugh at the poutiness to his voice, but my husband had just about walked in on us doing...that. I fell into the wall trying to jump into my pants and grunted. Turning my back to Roman so I didn't have to know that he'd seen that, I finished tugging them on and ran my fingers through my hair.

"Megan? Is that you?"

I turned, but Roman was already opening the door. I couldn't see around Roman, but judging by the startled yelp, Dylan had just come face to face with him. *Fuck.*

19

MEGAN

"Who the hell are you and what are you doing in my house?" Dylan demanded to Roman, like he wasn't an entire head and a half shorter than the man.

I stuck my head under Roman's arm and held out my hands, not wanting the weirdness to escalate to something worse. "What are you doing back in *my* house, Dylan?"

Dylan acted as though he'd been slapped. His head jerked back when he saw me, and his face pinched as though he'd been sucking on a lemon. "You… What were you doing in there, Megan?"

"Something private that you interrupted." Roman's voice was a pure growl, the heat that always radiated off him growing stronger.

"Excuse me?" Dylan gathered himself quickly. "That's my *wife* you're talking about."

I squeezed out of the door, planting myself in front of a very angry Roman. "Maybe we should take this downstairs?"

"Fine." Dylan stomped down the stairs, shooting dark glances back at us periodically.

I looked back at Roman and winced. He was not happy. "I don't know what he's doing back here."

He looked over my face, like he was searching for something, and sighed. "I know."

"This is so awkward. I didn't think I'd have to face off with him in front of you." I looked up at the ceiling and groaned.

"You would prefer me to leave?"

The hurt in his voice surprised me, almost as much as the alarm I felt at the thought of him leaving. "No! No. I'm not saying that."

He rolled his shoulders and blew out a breath. "Good."

"Okay." I nodded and turned to the stairs. "I guess we just go down there and see what he wants?"

With a hand on the center of my back, Roman led me down the stairs and into the kitchen. Dylan was looking through the liquor cabinets, slamming doors when he couldn't find anything.

"Yeah, empty. But you should know. You cleaned it out completely." I crossed my arms over my chest and prayed for strength.

Dylan scowled and pointed at Roman. "What is he still doing here?"

Roman growled, something I realized he was prone to doing, and actually curled his lip and bared his teeth at Dylan. It should've been weird, but it actually looked rather natural on him. It was, however, scary as hell. Probably more so when it was directed your way.

"Dylan, what are *you* doing here?"

"I live here, Megan."

I scoffed. "No, actually you don't. You literally don't. All of your stuff—and some of mine, I might add—has been removed."

He glared at Roman but didn't say anything else to him. "That wasn't me. It was Brandi. She told me I should take everything and I fell for it, Megan. I can't tell you how sorry I am."

I scrunched up my face in confusion, suddenly feeling as though I'd been teleported to an alternate reality. "What are you talking about?"

"*She* took everything. Apparently, it was her way of paying me back for not telling her about you." He looked away. "I don't know what came over me. I just had a hankering for something different, or so I thought. She wasn't it, though. I want you back, Megan. You're my wife. We've been together for twelve years. We shouldn't let anyone else get between us."

My brain reeled. "She took everything?"

"The money, the stuff, all of it. I woke up this morning to a rude note. She split—took it all. I came back here immediately when I realized the mistake I'd made. I knew right away I'd messed up."

"You knew 'right away'—after you woke up and she'd cleaned you out and dumped you?"

"Well, I knew yesterday."

I shook my head and sat down on one of the barstools. "Dylan, you stole from the business, left me to board up this home and the shop myself, took things from this house that didn't belong to you, and that's not even the worst! You've also been cheating on me for who knows how long, and when you left me to pick up your slack, I was nearly killed."

"Yeah, you stupid sonofabitch. I found her half-drowned in the ocean." Roman shook, his big hands balled up on the counter next to me. "The only reason I haven't snapped your scrawny ass in half yet is out of respect for Megan."

"Who the hell are you?!" Dylan tempted fate. "And why are you still here?"

"Stop. Dylan, you need to leave. You don't live here anymore. That was your choice, and I am not taking you back."

"Oh, I should have known. Just like your parents, huh? Give up on marriage at the first sign of trouble, is that it, Megan? You won't even honor our marriage by giving me another chance?"

I froze. Dylan was playing his trump card, and it felt like a gut punch. As if that wasn't enough, the icing on the cake was when he pulled out his wallet and slid across a picture of the two of us on our first date.

"I still carry this. I still love you. I don't care if you slept with him. I don't care. We can get past all of this. We can rebuild the shop. I'll do my part. I'll do more than my part. You deserve more."

I closed my eyes and shook my head harder.

"Megan, please. We can make it work. I *know* you don't want to follow in your mom's shoes. You give up on me, how long until you give up on the next guy? And the next? How many more men will you go through, just like her? It's easy to walk away, but anything worth having is worth fighting for."

I opened my eyes and the first thing I saw was Roman's hands. Still balled up, still tight, the veins strained. He was clearly holding himself back. He wanted to punch Dylan, I knew. Yet, he didn't. He was just waiting—giving me the chance to be in control.

My heart pounded. Dylan was right about one thing. I was willing to throw everything I'd worked at for the past twelve years away for a chance with Roman. Looking at him, touching him, was such an uplifting experience, it was like magic. Yes, I felt like there was magic happening when I was next to him. He was everything I admired. He behaved honorably to others, and to me as well. He said kind words to me, and his actions backed those words up. I'd never been treated so well by anyone before.

Could it be real, though? How long could it last? How was it possible that a man like Roman wanted to enter into a long-term relationship with me? It wasn't that I lacked self-esteem entirely, but I wasn't blind, either. He was stunning. I was...average.

He suddenly swore from beside me. Looking down at his watch, he swore again and then shot a deadly glare at Dylan. "I have to leave. I will be back."

"Don't bother."

Roman eased me off the stool and, with an arm around my waist, pulled me to the door with him. "Something's going down at the office. It's urgent or I wouldn't dream of leaving right now. Don't make any decisions while I'm gone. Please. I can see the wheels in your head turning and I know he's getting to you, but what he's saying is complete bullshit. He's trying to play you. You don't belong with him, Megan. You deserve so much better."

I felt like crying. I stared at my feet until Roman slid a finger under my chin and raised my head.

"Look at me. This I will promise you right now. If you chose me, there will not be another man after me. I'm not a twelve-year kind of guy. I'm a forever kind of guy. Just, please, wait for me to return."

I wanted to hold onto him, but he pressed a kiss to my forehead and was gone that fast, leaving me there with Dylan, who had no qualms about hitting below the belt to get me back.

There I was, the same large-stature woman with small breasts and big hips, who'd walked in on her husband as he went to town screwing his slender, beautiful mistress in our bed. A week later, I was still the same woman with a flabby belly and cellulite thighs, but now there were two men fighting over me. Life made zero sense.

20

ROMAN

I ripped the roof off the house without a strain. Throwing a slew of trashed shingles behind me, I growled and tugged at a beam that blocked my way in.

Roman! Calm yourself before you bring the entire house down on them!

I let out a wild roar in Serge's direction, unable to heed his command at that moment. I knew, deep down, that he was right. The family trapped in their bathroom could easily be crushed to death if I didn't handle the extraction delicately, but I was riled to the core.

Konstantin moved in next to me and grabbed a beam that was starting to slip. "Go!"

I lowered myself into the house and cleared a path headed in the direction of their screams. Dmitry and Alexei were right behind me, both offering support when the house shook. Serge grabbed me and yanked me backward just as I was about to pull the bathroom door open.

"Stop!" He jerked his chin up and gestured to the beam over the door. It was balancing precariously and would have undoubtedly cracked my skull if I'd followed through and opened the door.

The realization should have sobered me. It should have forced me to stop and pay closer attention to what I was doing. It didn't. I couldn't focus on anything other than the fact that I'd left my mate alone with a man who didn't deserve her but had a claim to her anyway. A man who was talking out his ass a mile a minute. It had been so obvious to me that he was saying whatever he thought would get the reaction he wanted from her, with no regard for the truth.

"You go and help Konstantin support the structure until we can get them out!"

I growled but did as I was told. My bear ripped at me, demanding to be let out. I knew exactly what he'd do—run back to Megan's house and tear her weasel of a husband to shreds. Unable to maintain control, I felt claws begin to extend from my fingertips.

"What the fuck happened, brother?"

I shook. I didn't know how much longer I could hold myself together.

Seconds later, the team emerged with the family—all injury-free. Good. We could get the hell out of there. The house didn't stand on its own for much longer, and as it collapsed in front of us, the family cried. The parents hugged their two children close and thanked us profusely for rescuing them and getting them all out safely.

My mind was elsewhere. I kept seeing Megan with that slimy little asshole. Would she buy into his manipulative bullshit? I knew he was only looking for someone to sponge off of and Megan had a heart of gold. He had nowhere to sleep and no money, but it was what he deserved. A taste of his own medicine. He'd had done to him exactly what he'd done to Megan. Karma. It pissed me off how he thought he could just waltz right back in and pick up where he left off.

I would dedicate myself to caring for Megan and respecting her needs and feelings. He never would. She didn't necessarily know that, though.

"You and me need to have a talk, Roman." Serge glared at me and pointed to the team's van. "Now."

The rest of the guys climbed into the back, as though that would give Serge and I any privacy. Not from shifter hearing, it wouldn't. I sat fuming, terrified that I might be losing my mate. I needed to get back there as soon as possible and fight for her.

"What the fuck is going on with you?"

"You know damn good and well what."

Serge nodded. He knew because he'd acted the same way when he met his mate. We'd been on a mission and he'd nearly blown the whole thing to hell after meeting Hannah. "I have a feeling. Mate?"

"Yeah."

The guys in the back cheered, but Serge growled. "What's the problem, then? And there is a problem, isn't there, Roman?"

I growled. "There is. She has...a husband. He left her, and she almost died because of his lack of concern." I released a slow breath. "He just came back. Says he's sorry. Says he loves her."

"Well, that explains why you almost got an entire family crushed to death."

"She's *my* mate. Mine. The fucker walks back in acting as though nothing ever happened. He's trying to trick her into thinking he cares and that she needs him."

Serge sighed. "Man, she's yours. No matter what the asshole says or does."

"What if she picks him?"

"She won't. It's not going to happen. If she's truly your mate, she's going to feel the same for you as you feel for her. She just won't understand it the same way. Non-shifters don't really listen to or trust their instincts the way we do. They also lie and deceive, so..." He shrugged. "I wish I'd have explained everything to Hannah earlier. It would've made things easier."

"Yeah, might I suggest you not give her your claiming mark until she understands why you do that?" Alexei called through the back glass.

Serge stepped on the brakes hard enough to nearly slam Alexei's face into the glass. "Shut the fuck up."

I looked out the front window, thinking. "Should I tell her? Everything?"

"Are you sure she's your mate?"

Scowling at him, I debated throttling him. "Are you sure Hannah is your mate?"

He snarled back at me. “Point taken.”

I sat there and tried to think it through. If she understood what was happening between us, maybe it would help her make her decision with more confidence. Maybe she would understand that we were meant to be together.

“Explain it to her. Just do it as gently as possible. It’s a lot for a human to take in.”

I nodded. “Let me out near Latte Love coffee shop.”

“Do I look like a chauffeur?”

“Serge.”

“Fine.”

I was nervous about revealing my shifter nature to Megan. She was my mate, though. That had to make it easier for her to understand everything. She was made for me, a shifter. That had to mean something.

When he stopped outside of Lotte Love, Serge clapped me on the shoulder. “Good luck, brother.”

“Give her your cub eyes if you have to.” Alexei grinned. “It works for me.”

“Shut up.” Dmitry punched him and shook his head. “She’s all yours, brother.”

I rolled my shoulders and walked toward her house. With each step, I felt more tense. I didn’t want to lose my mate before I even got the chance to show her what a life together would be like. Growling at myself, I broke into a run. This had to work.

21

MEGAN

I'd left Dylan in the kitchen while I started the generator and took a long, hot shower. I figured, what else could he steal? I emerged, to find that he'd lit candles and produced a bottle of wine from somewhere. When I came back to face him, he was in the shadows of candlelight. I flipped on the lights, willing to suck power from other things in the house to avoid sitting in the dark with him.

"Oh, okay. I just thought the candles added a nice ambiance." He crossed his ankle over his knee and stretched his arms out along the back of the couch, cockily sure of himself, which pissed me off.

"You can stay."

He grinned. "You're making the best choice, Megan. I—"

"ONLY until you find somewhere else to live." I balled my hands into fists to help me contain my emotions. "You'll need to figure something out with the bed in your room if you decide that staying here for the moment is best for you. It was damaged in the storm."

Sitting up, he shook his head. "Megan, let's talk about this."

"Okay."

"I apologized." He waited.

"And?"

"Well, I meant it. I am sorry. I shouldn't have gone the route that I did. I should've come to you when I felt dissatisfied."

I nodded and stared over his shoulder. "You should have. You didn't have to blindside me, Dylan. You didn't have to cheat, you didn't have to steal, and you didn't have to evacuate the island without the slightest concern for my safety or wellbeing."

"What do you want me to say here?"

"Nothing. There's nothing you can say. It's just as much my fault that it's come to this. I don't think I ever really saw you until this past week—not really. Every glance has been through rose-colored glasses. I've been in complete denial about the person I'd been living with—married to." I scrubbed my palms down my face. "We don't love each other. Maybe we used to, I'm not even sure. Did we just stop at some point? If we did, it was long before Brandi or Roman. If you loved me, you wouldn't have treated me so cruelly. If I loved you, it would've crushed me when you…well, you know. Honestly, though, Dylan, I feel relieved."

He leaned back on the couch, his kind expression replaced with one of disgust. "You feel *relieved*?"

"Yes. Relieved. Free. Like maybe I have a chance to actually be happy." I met his eyes. "I spent most of our marriage feeling inadequate and doing everything you wanted because I felt like I had to…to earn your love. I didn't think there was any other way because I wasn't pretty enough to keep you, or thin enough, so I figured I'd just bend over backward doing what you wanted for the rest of my life and that would ensure a long, happy marriage. You *let* me do that. You let me feel those things. And I wasn't happy at all."

"I didn't make you feel ugly."

"You never once told me I was beautiful—or attractive, even. You didn't call me pretty or tell me that you liked the way I looked. You wouldn't even touch my stomach."

He scowled and sat forward again. "So, it's all my fault?"

"No. It's not. But you pulled some massive shit this last week, Dylan, and that really opened my eyes. Even if I wanted to forgive you, I'd never be able to, not fully. I'd never stop looking over my shoulder to see if you were fucking someone else, or stealing from me, or setting me up to pull the rug out from under me again."

"This is bullshit, Megan."

"What did you think was going to happen? Honestly."

"You don't have to be a bitch."

I raised my eyebrows. "I'm being serious. Tell me what you honestly thought was going to happen when you walked back in here today. Talk me through it."

"I thought you'd fucking be glad that your husband came back. Instead, you were already spreading your legs for the first guy who wandered by. Didn't take you long."

"For the sake of argument, I'm going to ignore the fact that you're being a condescending ass, and ask you why you thought I'd be glad you were back. After what you did." I shook my head. "I was seconds from drowning. You left with zero regard for me. Instead of helping me and the two of us both getting out of here safely, you cleaned me out and ran off with your mistress. I nearly died trying to secure the house and the business. Is any of this sinking in?"

"Come on. You're not serious."

"Yes, I am. I got caught in a rip current and swept out to sea. I couldn't stay afloat. The last thing I remember was panicking when I realized I was going to die. Do you want to know what went through my head in those final moments?"

For a change, he looked slightly shaken. "What?"

"I was thinking about how easy it would be for you. If I died. No messy divorce, no prenup, no embarrassment. You'd just get a nice lump sum of life insurance money and get to run off with your Brandi."

"That's not… I… Megan, I wouldn't prefer you dead."

"I was so angry, thinking that I'd made it easier for you. You don't deserve anything else from me. You've taken more than you deserve already. Still, I feel like it's only right to be decent." I blew out a rough breath. "And that's the only reason I'm going to let you stay under my roof until you get your life together. I'll call the lawyers in the morning and get them started on the divorce papers. If you do decide to stay here, you're going to need to stay out of my way and don't bother me. We should probably talk about a timeline, too. My hospitality does not extend indefinitely. I suggest you find a job as soon as possible and then look for a place of your own."

"Megan, don't do this. I have nothing else." For once, there was emotion in his eyes. "I'm sorry I did all of this to you. I'm sorry about Brandi. I'm really sorry. I'll change. I'll do whatever you want. Just, please, don't make me start over."

"You did it to yourself. Don't make me out to be the bad guy. I'm going to go out and get some fresh air." I steeled myself against his hang-dog expression and walked away.

I pulled the door shut behind me and leaned against it. My heart was hammering in my chest and I felt nauseous. Why? Why did I feel like the villain? I wasn't being mean to Dylan. I was standing up for myself for a change. My patterning told me that I should comfort him, placate him, please him even if that meant being unfair to myself. It was hell to get out of that old way of thinking. The truth was that I wasn't leaving Dylan. I wasn't walking out on *him*. He had already walked out and left *me*. The only reason he'd come back with his lame attempt at groveling was that it hadn't worked out with his mistress and he had nowhere else to go for the moment. It had nothing to do with his feelings for me. He was a user, and I had been an enabler.

I walked down to the beach and sat in the sand just inches from the water's reach. I was still mad at it for trying to kill me. I figured it would be a while longer before I could wade back out into it without my mind reliving its force as it dragged me under.

Wasn't that just life, though? It knocked you down, and you had to take a moment before you had the strength to get back up and have another go at it. Was it crazy to even be thinking of starting something new with Roman when I was still reeling from Dylan's betrayal? If it was too soon, would I just get sucked back underwater?

22

MEGAN

"Hey."

I glanced over my shoulder at Roman and forced a smile. "Hey, yourself."

He sat next to me in the sand and stared out at the Atlantic, too. "Crazy to think that it's the same ocean that tried to take you away from me last night."

I looked away, afraid to let him see the tears well in my eyes. I buried my fingers in the sand and rested my cheek on my knee.

"I have something I need to tell you." He sighed. "You're probably going to think I'm crazy, but please hear me out."

My stomach twisted. "What?"

"I want to be with you. I want it so desperately that I can't think of anything else. I know it probably sounds insane to you. We met less than twenty-four hours ago, but I know that you are the woman I was meant to be with." He turned to face me full on. "My people…they just know when they meet 'the one.' Our soulmate."

My stomach twisted tighter. "Your people? Russians?"

"No. I'm not…normal, Megan. I'm sorry if it all sounds ridiculous and I'm just blurting it all out like this, but I need you to know. I need you to know about me before you make a decision."

"What are you talking about, Roman?"

"Shapeshifters. My people are shapeshifters. We have the ability to shift—to transform—into bears. Polar bears, to be specific." He paused. "I'm a polar bear shifter from Siberia, and you're my soulmate."

My heart sank, plummeted right to my feet. "Shapeshifters. Polar bears."

"Yeah. I know it probably sounds crazy to you, but we're real. I'm real. And so are soulmates. I am one hundred percent sure that you and I are made for each other. We're meant to be together."

I blinked a few times, unsure of how to react to everything he was laying at my feet. "Um… You're a polar bear shifter, and I was made for you."

"I know it's a lot to digest. You might even think I'm off my rocker right now. I can show you, though. I'll shift into my bear if it'll help, Megan. Let me prove it to you. Let me fight for you the way you deserve to be fought for."

I was going to cry. I just felt physically ill. "Can I think about it?"

Roman sat back, his face crestfallen. "You already chose him."

I shook my head. "No. He's leaving. It's definitely over between us."

"But you haven't chosen me, either."

I bit my lip hard and shook my head again. "I just need time to think."

"This was too much, huh?" He looked crushed, and the contrast between the true devastation on his face and the irritation that had shone on Dylan's made this all that much harder. But he was obviously insane.

I nodded and squeezed my eyes shut.

"Fuck. I'm sorry. Come here." His voice sounded heavy with emotion as he pulled me into his arms and held me against his chest. "I'm thinking of myself, and you're going through the end of your marriage. I'm sorry, Megan. I won't pressure you. I promise."

I dug my fingers into his shirt and held on, desperate for things to be different. He clearly had serious mental issues. I couldn't pursue anything with him. I wasn't going to drown again. Yet, it hurt.

Walking away, saying goodbye to him was harder than walking away from my twelve-year marriage.

He held me as I cried, his arms wrapped tightly around me. He murmured softly into my hair and cradled me through my tears. Damn, I felt so safe in his arms. Why did I have to fall for someone with such huge issues?

He apologized again and again, but he didn't beg me to change my mind. When I'd finished crying and pulled back, he let go. He didn't hide the sorrow in his own eyes, but he forced a smile for me. We stood up, and he pressed one last kiss to my forehead before standing rooted to the spot as he watched me walk away.

I couldn't go back to the house. I was in no mood to face Dylan. Instead, I walked past the house and through the sand dunes that separated Main Street from the residential area. On Main Street, I headed toward the shop, keeping my head down until I got there.

Not knowing what else to do, I plopped down on the concrete in front and stared at the crumpled wreckage. My whole life had been completely upended this week.

I was all cried out, so I just sat there relatively numb. The sun had set, the island was in darkness, and I wasn't sure where to go. Sunkissed Key suddenly felt suffocating.

I needed to scram. My mom had a place in Miami. It wouldn't take me long to get there, provided Matilda hadn't wrought too much damage along the way. It was a perfect plan, a chance to get away and to get my head on straight again.

As I headed back home, I saw Cameron Patrick lying in her hammock, her cat in her lap, and let myself in through her open patio door. "Cameron?"

She jumped, sending her cat skittering away. "Megan! You scared the living tar right out of me!"

"Sorry."

"What's up?"

"I can't stay here on the island. Dylan's back and I need to put some distance between us. I lost my SUV to the storm. Any chance I could borrow your car for a few days?"

She sat up gracefully and came over to me. "Oh, honey, yes."

"I wouldn't ask if it wasn't an emergency."

"Stop. It's fine. You know I walk everywhere anyway. Take the car for as long as you need. I'm not going anywhere unless another hurricane happens along." She hugged me tightly and then pulled me into her house. "Where are you going? Somewhere safe, I hope?"

"My mom's."

She patted her chest. "Good. Just be good to yourself, honey. You deserve some pampering, you really do."

I nodded and took the keys she handed me. "Thank you, Cameron. I'll repay you when I get back."

"Nonsense. Go on, now. Get out of here. I've got plans with that hammock tonight and they don't involve you." She pushed me toward the garage door and flashed me a smile. "Be safe."

I settled into her car and backed out after hitting the garage button. Minutes later, I was on the highway, heading north to the mainland and some breathing room.

23

ROMAN

"I understand what you're going through, Roman, but I need you to drag your mopey ass somewhere else. Kerrigan has been trying to get into that drawer behind you for the last hour."

I looked up at Serge and blinked. "Huh?"

"Move, brother." He gestured toward Kerrigan and shook his head. "You're in her way, but she's not going to be bold enough to ask you to move."

"I would've asked...eventually."

I scooted out of the way and looked around. What was I supposed to be doing? "Any jobs for me?"

Kerrigan, P.O.L.A.R.'s new dispatcher shook her head and gestured to Serge.

I looked at Serge. "You're still not giving me anything?"

"No can do. You're not in the right headspace. Until you're able to focus on a task, sending you out will make you a liability to yourself and others."

Kerrigan smiled at me, a gentle smile that someone might give to a feeble grandparent or a sick child. "Maybe there are smaller tasks that need doing? If you're feeling up to it."

Serge shook his head. "Nope."

"Fuck, man. What do you want me to do?" I stood up, sending my chair flying into the cabinet behind me. "I'm going crazy."

"Outside. Take it outside." Dmitry stood up and pointed at the door.

Serge gave him a weird look and shook his head. "He's right. Come on, brother. Outside with me."

I stomped out the door and looked around, the same way I did every time I stepped outside. I was hoping to see Megan. It'd been over a month since I'd last seen her that day on the beach and it was killing me. Even if she didn't choose me, I just wanted to see her and make sure that she was okay and happy.

"Go after your mate, Roman. This isn't going to resolve itself until you do."

I growled and shoved him, my anger boiling to the surface. "You think this is my choice? You think I don't want to go to her every second of every day?!"

He shoved me back. "I don't know! All you're doing is sitting around, mopey-assed and bitchy about it."

I drew back my fist and slammed it into his jaw before I even thought twice about it. It felt so good, I almost did it again, until Serge ducked and hit me with an uppercut that sent me flying backward into the side of the building. That felt good, too. After feeling nothing but deep sorrow for a month, I was ready to trade it some good old anger.

I went for him again and he was there, ready for me. He took my punches and gave back just as good as he got. Rolling around on the ground, we tussled until we were too tired to keep going.

Flat on my back on the sandy ground, I looked up at the sky and swore. "I don't know why I just blurted it all out to her like that."

Serge sat up. "We told you to. Sure, maybe you could've had a little more finesse about it, but we all thought it was the right way to go, man."

"This is killing me. Literally."

"I was there. When I couldn't get Hannah to talk to me, I thought I was dying, and that was only for a couple of days. I feel for you. I really do. You can't just give up, though."

"I haven't." I sat up and looked out at the ocean. "I go by her house every night to see if she's back. She's not. Her jackass of a husband—"

"Ex-husband, from what I hear."

"Yeah. Ex-husband. He's still there. The fucker hasn't done a thing to the place. It still has damage from the storm. You'd think he'd at least make the repairs since he's staying there. I'd really like to tear him to pieces and feed him to the sharks. Hell, maybe if I did, she'd come home."

"No hurting humans—if you can help it. Just remember that."

I dug my fingers into the sand and scowled. "She's got to come back. She has to."

"She will. And then things will work themselves out. You're mates. That means something." He stood up. "If you hit me again, I'm going to have the rest of the guys beat your ass, though."

I waved him off and sighed. Looking back out at the water, I wondered for the millionth time where she was. I wanted to believe Serge was right, but I wasn't so sure. I'd somehow managed to fuck things up so royally. I shouldn't have told her. I should've just waited until she trusted me more. I hadn't been thinking, though. I was so afraid of losing her to that asshole's manipulation that I'd jumped the gun and scared her.

Everything in me felt like it was closing down—dying. Now that I'd met her, I found living without her pointless. I wanted to come home to her smiling face, and taste the sweetness of her lips. I wanted to be the one to comfort her when she was upset and build her back up when she was feeling down. I wanted her to be the one I shared my day with. I wanted to indulge in simple things that I hadn't thought mattered before her.

The kicker was that the heat didn't bother me anymore. While the other guys still sweated in front of the crappy AC unit, I couldn't care less. What did it matter that I was a little physically uncomfortable when the real pain was lodged deep in my heart?

I swore and dragged myself to my feet. I had to do something, anything. I was slowly going insane. Without anything better to do, I decided that it was time to take out her trash.

I couldn't hurt her fuckface ex-husband, but Serge hadn't said anything about scaring the shit out of him.

24

MEGAN

"Hello?" I let myself into the house and prepared myself for coming face to face with my now ex-husband. "Dylan?"

I hadn't talked to him since the lawyers fast-tracked the divorce for me. I wasn't looking forward to it.

But all that met me was silence and an empty house. I looked around before breathing a huge sigh of relief. It appeared that Dylan was gone. There was nothing of his anywhere in the house and the entire place had been cleaned and put in order. The window in the bedroom was fixed, and even the destroyed mattress had been hauled away.

Back downstairs, I sank into the couch. That was a big weight off my shoulders. I closed my eyes, letting the silence envelop me.

My mother's house was never quiet. Mom had been living in Miami lately since her newest husband, Jerry, wanted to be closer to his middle-school-aged daughter, especially after the hurricane scare. Mom was always yelling at the poor hired help. Jerry was always yelling at his daughter, and the daughter was always just yelling.

Then, there were the parties. Mom was a social butterfly when it came to parties. She even threw one for my divorce, much to my dismay. She invited all of her socialite friends, and I saw way more than my fair share of drug use and weird sex that night. Apparently, divorce parties made the jet set frisky.

I should've left and gotten myself a nice, quiet hotel room after the first night, but it had still been hard to be alone with my thoughts. I'd even become good friends with one of her gardeners, a middle-aged guy named Emmett. We snuck into the shed during my divorce party and played gin rummy all night long. Anything to avoid being alone.

Being alone meant I would be obsessing over Roman. I still had dreams about him every night. I woke up hot and bothered and tangled in sweaty sheets. And it was only getting worse! There wasn't anything that didn't make me think of Roman. I had to make up some phony excuse for my middle-school-aged stepsister as to why the documentary we were watching about polar bears made me cry.

The only reason I'd finally decided to return home was that the divorce was finalized and it was time to stand up to Dylan and take my life back. I couldn't hide forever.

Sitting on my couch, I now wondered if I'd returned too soon. The silence already felt heavy. I needed to face things, though, like an adult.

I headed up to the guestroom to shower and get ready for bed. Wearing a new nightgown that Mom had bought me, I slipped between the sheets and tried to think of anything other than the last night I'd been in the same bed, and the handsome man who'd been showering me with attention.

It was too early to sleep, just after sunset, but I really didn't know what else to do, and now that I'd returned, the thoughts of Roman were becoming even more overwhelming. A month should've been enough time to work the guy out of my system. I'd blinked and been over Dylan. Why couldn't I do the same with Roman, who I had only known for a day?

My phone rang from my pants pocket on the floor and I ignored it. When the ringing started up again, I leaned over and fished it out. "Hello?"

"Hey, baby girl! Did you get home okay?" My mom sounded tipsy already.

"Yeah, Mom. I'm home."

"Is that asshole still there?"

"No, actually. He's gone. The house is clean, too, which was completely unexpected. I thought I'd find it destroyed." I settled back against my pillow and stared up at the ceiling. "Everything okay there?"

"Well, yes. We're just missing you." She paused. "Sweetie?"

"Yeah, Mom?"

"The best way to get over Dylan is to just jump back into the dating pool. Go out on a date and have some fun. You're beautiful and there's no reason you should sit around moping and wasting your best years."

I just rolled my eyes. "Okay, Mom."

"I'm serious. Put on your best Spanx and one of those little dresses I got you."

"The nightgowns?"

"Yes! Aren't they just the cutest?"

"You want me to go out in a nightie to get a date?"

"Why not? You're young and free, Megan. Oh, to be single and in my early thirties again…"

"Okay, Mom. I need to go." Before she could scar me permanently, I hung up and turned my ringer off. I didn't need any more unsolicited advice from my mother.

I closed my eyes and played the counting sheep game, which actually worked. It didn't keep me asleep for long, though. I awoke with a start a few hours later and realized I'd been dreaming about Roman again.

I got up and stretched, knowing that I'd had about all the sleep I was going to get that night. My mind was spinning. I wondered what Roman was doing. Had he moved on? Had he just told me that stuff about being a polar bear to scare me off because he wanted to get away from me, or did he really believe that he was a shapeshifter?

They were the same questions I'd asked myself over and over again, but they were always freshest on my mind after a dream. The dreams were usually of a massive snow-white bear walking beside me, but I was never scared of it. It was my protector. It was Roman.

I walked downstairs and had just passed the windows that looked out over the ocean when I froze. "You're absolutely losing it, Megan."

Slowly, I backed up. I looked out the window again and felt my heart skip a beat. Something was in the water. Something large and white and much bigger than a person. My stomach fluttered, and I gasped when I got a really good look at it. It was a bear. A huge, fucking polar bear.

Before I could even think through what I was doing, I was racing out of my house, down the stairs, across the sand, and plunging into the water. "Stop! Come back!"

Up to my hips, I moved harder, desperate. I had to know. The butterflies in my stomach swore that it was Roman. Had I lost my mind, too? There could not really be a polar bear swimming off the Florida Keys. "Roman!"

And then it was just a few feet away from me. Standing on its back feet in the water, it towered over me.

Its eyes. Those were the giveaway. A sob tore from my throat and I covered my mouth with my hands. It was definitely him.

A bear one second, Roman the next, he stood in the waves with me, just staring back at me. His face looked pained and hesitant. I don't know which one of us moved first, but a second later I was wrapped around him like a burrito.

If this was a dream, I didn't want to wake up.

25

MEGAN

I kissed him, desperate for the taste of him on my lips. I grasped his face and then his head and neck as I deepened the kiss. His hair was longer under my fingers, his beard thicker against my face. I'd missed him so much. I locked my legs around his waist and cried. "You aren't crazy!"

We were moving through the water, the waves hitting me lower and lower until we were out of them. Roman gripped me with one hand under my ass and the other braced around my back. "Why would you run into the ocean toward a bear?"

I might have taken offense to the tone of his question if he wasn't kissing me back in between words. I tilted my head back when his lips moved to my throat. "I knew it was you. Why didn't you show me? All this time, I thought you had mental problems. Why didn't you make me believe you?"

We stumbled up a few steps and paused for a second. Roman's hands never stopped moving. "Stupid. I was so stupid."

I gasped as he bounced me higher and carried me the rest of the way up the stairs in his arms. He kicked the door closed behind us and sat me down on the kitchen island. The granite was cold under my ass, but Roman was there, stroking my throat with his tongue, pushing the nightgown straps down my shoulders.

"Tell me you're okay with this, Megan. Tell me you want me, too."

"I want you." I gasped as his mouth moved across my shoulder. "I'm more than okay with it. As long as you don't stop."

He growled and nipped my shoulder before pulling back and staring into my eyes. "I have to tell you a few more things before we do this. I want to make sure you know what you're getting into."

I bit my lip, needier than I'd ever felt. "Talk fast."

"I'm going to bite you."

I moaned and dropped my head back. "As in foreplay? I don't need it, Roman."

"I'm going to mark you. If you'll let me. My bear…he recognizes you, too, as our mate. I want to claim you as mine. Forever." He growled as my foot stroked up the back of his thigh. "Do you understand that? Forever, Megan."

I met his heated gaze and clarity washed over me. It was a clarity that ran deeper than his words. How it could be the easiest decision I'd ever made, I didn't know. It should've been harder, especially after Dylan, but it wasn't. "Forever."

He stepped back into me and kissed me fiercely. His hands worked my nightgown lower, exposing my bare breasts and stomach. As he kissed me, his fingertips traced up my sides and then down my back before lowering me back on the island.

I gasped at the cold granite, but it faded when I saw the way Roman was staring down at me. Heat—pure, unfiltered heat and need washed over me as I saw the same reflected back from him. He growled low in his throat and cupped my breasts. I arched my back and offered them up to him.

"Fuck, you're beautiful." He closed his mouth over one nipple and then the other, slowly torturing both of them until I writhed. He only pulled back to kiss down my stomach, dipping his tongue into my navel before ripping my nightgown down the middle, exposing my panties.

He pressed his mouth to me over the panties, his tongue hot and wet enough to drive me wild. His hair had grown long enough to grip, so I did. Pulling his face into me, I rolled my hips under his mouth. Roman yanked my panties down and quickly devoured me.

I screamed out an orgasm in seconds—faster than I wanted, but then he was lifting me into his arms and carrying me up the stairs. In my bedroom, he gently put me on the bed and then climbed over me.

"You're the one for me, Megan. The only woman for me." He kissed me slowly while lowering his body to mine.

"I haven't stopped thinking about you while I was gone. I missed you. I missed you as if I'd known you my whole life." I wrapped my arms and legs around him and gasped when his shaft rested against my core. "Roman."

He gripped my hips as he lifted himself and lined our bodies up. Then one of his hands grasped the hair at the back of my head as he slowly sank into me, inch by inch.

Clutching his shoulders, I let out a soft moan as he filled me completely. White hot pleasure tingled through me instantly and I rode out that wave until Roman pulled out and then sank back in. His mouth next to mine, our breath mingled. His eyes burned into me as he watched my reactions. Stroke by stroke, he drove us both higher.

His hands gripped me tighter, the one on my hip had moved to my thigh, and he reached between us to stroke that little bundle of nerves. My neck was stretched back and to the side by his hand in my hair and then his warm breath was fanning over my neck.

I felt him hesitate and knew that he was waiting for a signal from me that it was okay. It was more than okay. I needed it. I felt like I was going to snap into a million pieces if he didn't do it. I pulled his mouth down to my neck and moaned his name.

Roman sank his teeth into my neck—sharp pain that lasted for less than a second. Then a wave of immense pleasure rolled over me. Going under, I knew there would be no coming back up from what was consuming me. My body tightened painfully around him as I felt him swelling even larger inside me, exploding my world.

I came with a scream and a violent shudder. Everything I thought I knew about love was shattered by Roman. He growled against my neck as he came, and something powerful snapped into place between us as he did. Wild, desperate, we sought out each other's mouths and kissed as we both trembled from what had just happened.

I could feel a part of him, so deep within me that nothing would ever be able to remove it. Soul deep.

That quickly, I knew that everything he'd told me was true and that we *were* bound by fate, or whatever it was that drew us together. I could feel the bond between us like it was a real, tangible thread running between us.

It should've been embarrassing that I cried, but Roman just rolled us over and held me against his chest. Stroking my hair and whispering soothing words, he spoke to me with a hint of an accent that rarely came out, and I knew he was feeling emotional, too.

Roman had come into my life and rescued me with a force and speed that rivaled Matilda, and I would forever be his. And he would forever be mine.

26

ROMAN

"Your house isn't meant to hold me in my bear form, Megan." Standing in my mate's bathroom, I stood with my hands on my hips, staring at her with raised eyebrows. "It's not a good idea."

Megan, who'd come into her confidence after spending the last few days naked with me, stretched with her arms over her head, showing me every inch of her sexy feminine form. Her bottom lip poked out, and she batted her eyelashes at me. "Please?"

I swore. "Fine. It's your floor."

"Yeah, floors that I put in. They'll hold you." She pulled herself onto the counter and watched me with wide eyes. She really wanted to see my other form again.

Unwilling to fight her on it any longer, I shifted. The floor creaked under my weight, but she was right, it held. I filled every available space in the bathroom and then some. Looking down at Megan, I cocked my head to the side and sniffed at her.

Her eyes were wider than I'd ever seen them. She lowered herself to the floor and was instantly lost in my fur. "Ahh! Oh, my god!"

I shifted back, afraid I'd accidentally hurt her, but I found her giggling wildly. "You scared the shit out of me! Why'd you scream like that?"

She was laughing so hard, I thought she was crying. "I'm so sorry. I just got excited. You're so cuddly and soft."

"I'm not cuddly! I'm an apex predator, woman. Top of the food chain."

"Yeah, okay." Laughing again, she wiped at her eyes. "I'm sorry. I really am. I just… I can't stop thinking about how my mom had a dog when I was young who would pee on this fur rug she had."

I gave her a deadpan stare, unamused.

"I'm so sorry! I just…" She laughed harder, holding her side. "I want to take naps in your fur."

I tried to keep scowling, but her laughter and amusement were pleasing. I easily picked her up and threw her over my shoulder, slapping her ass as I did. "You're not very respectful of my deadly predator status."

She laughed wildly when I dropped her onto the bed and came down on top of her. I buried my face in her neck and growled. She instantly arched her back and rubbed her soft body against mine.

"I love you, Megan."

She froze and blinked up at me.

I just smiled, knowing that she loved me, too, whether she was ready to say it aloud or not. I could see it in the way she looked at me, and in the little things she did for me. I could feel it radiating off of her through our bond. Her feelings for me were as real as mine were for her. "I love you and I'm going to spend the rest of my life giving you everything you want. Naps in my fur, babies, anything."

Her eyes filled with tears, and she grabbed my neck to pull me down for a kiss. "I love you, too."

I rolled us over so she was on top of me. I felt my own wave of emotion at hearing the words. She wasn't holding anything back. She was giving every part of herself to me. "Yeah?"

She stroked her hands down my chest and bit her lip. "It's later, Roman."

For a second I didn't know what she meant, but then I remembered that first night we spent together in the bathtub. The promise that she could return the favor later. "It's later?"

She grinned. "It's later."

"Thank god for Florida." I gritted my teeth as my sexy little mate slid down my body seductively, licking her lips with her own eagerness to make later happen.

THE END

NEXT BOOK IN THIS SERIES

Substandard job performance,

Indebted to a sleazy loan shark,

Crushing on a shifter who's out of her league,

Kerrigan is in a heck of a pickle.

Dmitry's not gentle.

He's not the nurturing type.

He's a cold-blooded killer—a P.O.L.A.R. assassin

But, when he steps in to protect her, Kerrigan doesn't see a killer, she sees a Hero Bear.

Get Hero Bear HERE

BEARS OF BURDEN

In the southwestern town of Burden, Texas, good ol' bears Hawthorne, Wyatt, Hutch, Sterling, and Sam, and Matt are livin' easy. Beer flows freely, and pretty women are abundant. The last thing the shifters of Burden are thinking about is finding a mate or settling down. But, fate has its own plan...

1. Thorn
2. Wyatt
3. Hutch
4. Sterling
5. Sam
6. Matt

* * *

SHIFTERS OF HELL'S CORNER

In the late 1800's, on a homestead in New Mexico, a female shifter named Helen Cartwright, widowed under mysterious circumstances, knew there was power in the feminine bonds of sisterhood. She provided an oasis for those like herself, women who had been dealt the short end of the stick. Like magic, women have flocked to the tiny town of Helen's Corner ever since. Although, nowadays, some call the town by another name, ***Hell's Crazy Corner.***

1. Wolf Boss
2. Wolf Detective
3. Wolf Soldier
4. Bear Outlaw
5. Wolf Purebred

* * *

DRAGONS OF THE BAYOU

Something's lurking in the swamplands of the Deep South. Massive creatures exiled from their home. For each, his only salvation is to find his one true mate.

1. Fire Breathing Beast
2. Fire Breathing Cezar
3. Fire Breathing Blaise
4. Fire Breathing Remy
5. Fire Breathing Armand
6. Fire Breathing Ovide

* * *

RANCHER BEARS

When the patriarch of the Long family dies, he leaves a will that has each of his five son's scrambling to find a mate. Underneath it all, they find that family is what matters most.

1. Rancher Bear's Baby
2. Rancher Bear's Mail Order Mate
3. Rancher Bear's Surprise Package
4. Rancher Bear's Secret
5. Rancher Bear's Desire
6. Rancher Bears' Merry Christmas

Rancher Bears Complete Box Set

* * *

KODIAK ISLAND SHIFTERS

On Port Ursa in Kodiak Island Alaska, the Sterling brothers are kind of a big deal.
They own a nationwide chain of outfitter retail stores that they grew from their father's little backwoods camping supply shop.
The only thing missing from the hot bear shifters' lives are mates! But, not for long...

1. Billionaire Bear's Bride (COLTON)
2. The Bear's Flamingo Bride (WYATT)
3. Military Bear's Mate (TUCKER)

* * *

SHIFTERS OF DENVER

Nathan: Billionaire Bear- A matchmaker meets her match.
Byron: Heartbreaker Bear- A sexy heartbreaker with eyes for just one woman.
Xavier: Bad Bear - She's a good girl. He's a bad bear.

1. Nathan: Billionaire Bear
2. Byron: Heartbreaker Bear
3. Xavier: Bad Bear

Shifters of Denver Complete Box Set

Made in the USA
Coppell, TX
07 February 2020

15513811R00076